Lincolnshire

DM

DANGEROUS FLIRTATION

Rosalind thought she had her life all mapped out — a job she loved, a thoughtful, reliable fiancé . . . what more could she want? How was she to know that a handsome stranger with laughing blue eyes and a roguish grin would burst into her life, kiss her to distraction and turn her world upside down? But there was more to Jack Drayton than met the eye. He offered romance, excitement, and passion — and challenged Rosalind to accept. Dared she?

Books by Liz Fielding
in the Linford Romance Library:

HIS LITTLE GIRL
GENTLEMEN PREFER . . .
BRUNETTES

LIZ FIELDING

DANGEROUS FLIRTATION

Complete and Unabridged

LINFORD
Leicester

First published in Great Britain in 1994

First Linford Edition
published 2009

British Library CIP Data

Fielding, Liz.
   Dangerous flirtation- -
   (Linford romance library)
   1. Love stories.
   2. Large type books.
   I. Title II. Series
   823.9'14–dc22

   ISBN 978–1–84782–830–9

Published by
F. A. Thorpe (Publishing)
Anstey, Leicestershire

Set by Words & Graphics Ltd.
Anstey, Leicestershire
Printed and bound in Great Britain by
T. J. International Ltd., Padstow, Cornwall

This book is printed on acid-free paper

1

Rosalind Parry pushed the tenancy agreement away and sat back in her chair. She felt restless, all at odds with herself, and checking the clauses of the agreement suddenly seemed a very tedious way to be spending her birthday. She picked up the expensive card that stood on her desk and read the message once more. 'To Rosalind, best wishes for a happy birthday, Anthony.' Not the world's most romantic message. But then Anthony was not the world's most romantic man.

She shook herself. What on earth was she thinking about? Indulging in a fit of self-pity because the man in her life hadn't rushed in this morning, kissed her silly and given her a bunch of roses? The thought of Anthony doing anything so unrestrained raised her generous mouth into a truant smile that she

1

quickly retrieved with a tiny stab of guilt. He would never do anything so ridiculous. That was one of things she liked most about him. Her father had been the one for grand gestures. Expensive impulses. Wild fancies. Excesses of emotion. And she knew only too well where they had led. She replaced the card, very carefully. That wasn't for her. She liked everything just the way it was. Romance was for fools. Anthony might not bring her roses, but she knew he would always be there when she needed him. That was worth a ton of roses.

She picked up the document and tried to concentrate, but the words danced around the page and refused to make sense. It wasn't as if he had *forgotten* her birthday, she reminded herself, and glanced again at the card that had been waiting for her this morning. Knowing he would be out of the office most of the day, he had taken the trouble to leave his card on her desk last night so that she would find it first thing this morning. The sort of thoughtful gesture that she appreciated. And they were going to a concert this evening. She sighed a little. If she was brutally honest with herself, it was the thought of the concert that was depressing her. She enjoyed classical music, not quite with Anthony's earnestness it was true, but tonight it was Shostakovich. She would try to enjoy it for Anthony's sake, but it wouldn't be easy.

At least the choice of restaurant had been left to her. Anthony had pulled a face when she had asked to be taken to the new French restaurant in the town centre, but it had been her birthday treat, she reminded herself when she had almost lost her nerve at his puzzled, 'Are you quite sure?' and he had shrugged and smiled a little and said that she should be indulged since it was her birthday.

And she was almost certain that tonight he would suggest they set a date for the wedding. He had thought she was a little young to rush into marriage.

But she was twenty-four today. Surely not too young for anything. Even marrying a man fifteen years older than herself.

A sudden quietness in the office dragged her thoughts back to her immediate surroundings and made her look up from her apparent deep concentration on the document before her. There was someone standing in front of her desk, someone dressed in a pair of well-worn denims that at her eye-level stretched tightly across a pair of arrogant hips. For a moment her gaze was fixed there. She swallowed, the faintest flush warming her cheeks and forced her eyes upward. A black T-shirt clung to his body, outlining the sculptured muscles of his chest. Her eyes seemed to rise forever until, above the strong, tanned column of his neck she met a pair of eyes so blue that they might have been plucked from the summer sky.

'Yes?' she asked, hoarsely, cleared her throat and tried again. 'Can I help you?'

He smiled slowly, the corners of his mouth creasing, strong white teeth sparkling against a warm, sensuous mouth. It was only then, as he lifted the instrument to his mouth, that she saw the saxophone in his hand. She gasped as the first notes of music whispered into the waiting silence of the office. She had heard the simple tune a thousand times, sung at numberless birthday parties, but never played like this.

Strong fingers teased the keys, tormenting the mellow sound that spiralled upwards, soaring dangerously higher and higher until Rosalind caught her breath on a top note held endlessly, balancing on the razor-edge of destruction. When she thought the sound must shatter and destroy them all, the musician, the instrument, the stunned listeners, it slid back into the depths along a slow, beautiful scale that subsided into a note so blue that she could have cried. The tune had been taken apart by a master and put back together again, then left for lesser mortals to make of it what they would.

While she sat, weak to the bone, he leaned across her desk and removed the dark-rimmed spectacles from her nose and dropped them on the desk, regarding her with the slightest frown. For a moment nothing happened. Then, without warning he captured the back of her head in one strong hand and bent to kiss her. His mouth moved over hers as sweet as his music, heartbreaking as the blues and she was lost.

'Rosalind!'

She jumped at the sound of her name and their lips parted. For a moment the stranger continued to hold her, his face inches from her own. 'Happy birthday, Rosalind Parry,' he murmured.

'What on earth is going on here?' the indignant voice persisted, and the stranger finally released her, straightened and turned slowly to glance down at the furious figure of Anthony Harlowe. His scornful appraisal took in the smoothly tailored grey three-piece suit, the hair carefully brushed to conceal a thinning spot, the outraged expression.

'Who the devil are you?' he asked, with a casual insolence that drew a sharp, anguished breath from Rosalind.

Anthony's face darkened ominously. 'I am Anthony Harlowe, a partner in this firm. And this young woman is my fiancée,' he added, without a very strict regard for the truth.

The man glanced back at Rosalind and she saw the measuring look, the slight tightening at the corners of his mouth as he sought in vain for a ring. 'Is she?' he asked, softly. His eyes held hers and she knew the question was for her, not Anthony. He wrenched his eyes from Rosalind's and turned back to the furious figure beside him. 'Then I suggest you put up an 'under offer' notice without delay if you want to discourage viewing. That is what estate agents do, isn't it?' he enquired politely, but he didn't wait for an answer.

'Although I would have thought a diamond more usual under these particular circumstances. Meanwhile, Anthony Harlowe, I had a special request to wish the young lady many happy returns of the day.' His eyes returned to hers. 'She didn't object, so I don't see why you should.'

Rosalind thought she might die of shame, hoped the floor would simply open up and swallow her. She hadn't asked this man to kiss her, but she hadn't stopped him. Hadn't wanted him to stop. She had cooperated more than willingly in an embrace that suddenly appeared to be threatening everything she wanted. Well, she wouldn't let it happen. Not while there was a chance to retrieve the situation.

She stood up quickly and slipped her arm through Anthony's, knowing full well that he disliked any sort of public demonstration of affection, but sensing instinctively that he would not object on this occasion. Nevertheless, she kept her fingers firmly crossed. Behind

Anthony, the stranger's mouth twisted in a knowing parody of a smile that mocked her and she looked quickly away. She saw that the rest of the staff were grinning behind their desks and knew in an instant what had happened.

'It was just a joke, Anthony.' She turned to the man, relief oddly tinged with disappointment. 'A kiss-o-gram? Is that what they call it?' His dress was casual enough, but there was something about him that suggested power, authority, not this rather seedy existence. 'Do you do this for a living?' she asked, suddenly quite angry, she wasn't sure whether with him or with herself for believing he had meant that dizzying kiss.

He raised one well-marked brow, his wry expression momentarily disconcerting her, before answering her question with one of his own. 'Do you think I should?'

'I really have no idea what you should do,' she answered, quickly.

'No? Well, I thought I'd ask. Since

you obviously enjoyed it so much.' Rosalind recognised the brazen challenge behind his eyes, daring her to deny it and dark colour seared her cheeks.

Anthony glared at the man, letting his eyes run scathingly over the black T-shirt, the denim jacket, the saxophone. 'I think it's time you left.'

The blue eyes hardened as his attention returned to the indignant man at his elbow and then smiled slightly as if he found the situation amusing. 'I understood Miss Parry was the manager here.'

Anthony's lips thinned. He had not missed the hectic colour on Rosalind's cheeks, nor the undercurrent of tension that had sparked between them. He detached himself from Rosalind. 'I'll see you in my office, Rosalind.' He turned, glared around the office and half a dozen pairs of eyes quickly found something more interesting to look at, then walked stiffly to the stairs which led to the partners' suite above the main branch of the largest firm of estate agents in the city of Melchester and its adjacent county.

Apparently unconcerned that he was wreaking havoc in her office, with her relationship with Anthony, the man turned back to Rosalind. 'Have you any requests?' He put the sax to his lips and began to tease out the first notes of 'Rhapsody in Blue'.

'No!' She put out a hand to stop him and the music came to an abrupt halt as her fingertips grazed his wrist. She withdrew her hand abruptly. He waited, apparently expecting an explanation. 'I'm sorry, you really must go. I . . . I'm sorry,' she repeated, embarrassed by Anthony's rudeness, needing to say something to correct whatever impression she had given the man. She wasn't the sort of girl who allowed every good-looking man she met to kiss her, but her voice trailed away under his impudent stare.

'What are you most sorry for?' he asked, with interest. 'Being kissed, or enjoying it?' His eyes narrowed on her sharp intake of breath. 'Or both?'

'I . . . ' Her mouth dried. 'You were simply doing what you were paid for. I'm afraid Anthony was unnecessarily rude.'

'Was he?' He took her left hand and stared at it for a moment. 'If he's really going to marry you, I'd say he was pretty restrained under the circumstances. Or maybe he's simply hoping?' Rosalind was fervently wishing she had simply followed Anthony to his office, but now this man was standing in her way. Taking advantage of the fact that he had her trapped in her corner at the rear of the office, he reached out and caught a strand of dark copper-coloured hair that had strayed from its pins when he kissed her. He tucked it gently back into place, his hand remaining there, the touch of his fingertips at her temple intoxicating as champagne.

'Please go!' she hissed.

'Let me take you out to dinner tonight.'

'Don't be ridiculous!'

His fingers slid down the smooth line of her jaw, tilted her chin so that she was forced to meet his eyes, and she seemed powerless to move, stop this madness. 'I don't think there's anything ridiculous about asking a beautiful girl out to dinner,' he murmured, softly. 'And you know you want to come.' He was making love to her, right there in the office, with his voice, his eyes, the sensuous curve of his mouth.

The front office doorbell clanged and she jerked around startled by the sound and was immediately aware of a number of faces still trained in undisguised fascination on the pair of them. The knowledge was like a bucket of cold water, shocking her back from the edge of madness. She straightened her jacket, fastened the buttons in an attempt to restore her sense of control. 'You'd better go or I'll have no choice but to call Security,' she said, painfully aware that her voice was little more than a breath.

A smile, gentle even in its mockery, curved his full sensuous lower lip. 'I think it's a little late for that. A bit like locking the stable door after the horse has bolted.' He propped her spectacles back on her nose and pushed them up until she was almost restored to her usual prim appearance. But she didn't feel prim. The plain grey suit, the high-necked blouse did nothing to help. Her breasts strained against the soft cloth, her mouth felt hot and swollen and she was certain that her hair was all over the place. Her heartbeat was in chaos and she could feel the pulse at her throat throbbing almost painfully as a result of her impetuous response to the man standing before her. 'Now, what time shall I pick you up?' he asked.

'I'm going out this evening. Please, you must go.' This time she didn't wait for his agreement, but squeezed past him, closing her eyes as her body brushed against his to send tiny electric shocks through every nerve ending.

Then she walked quickly to the door, her back as straight as she could make it, knowing that every move was being eagerly watched. What on earth had she done? News of this would be in every branch by the end of the week. End of the week? She laughed a silent, scornful laugh at herself for placing the incident so low in the interest of every member of her office. Rather sooner than that, she thought.

The cool and very proper Miss Rosalind Parry had been kissed to distraction in front of her entire staff. If Anthony had forgotten himself sufficiently to kiss her in the office, the news would probably have caused a buzz of amusement to be passed on in conversation. But they had decided on a bit of fun for her birthday and she had provided them with a show beyond their wildest dreams. This was news too good to wait. Hands were already hovering over telephones waiting for her to disappear upstairs to Anthony's office so that they could spread the word to every branch office in the city.

At the entrance the tall figure turned and before she could prevent him he took her hand. 'Tomorrow, then.' He was insistent. 'Twelve-thirty in the wine bar across the road.' Conscious of their audience, she opened the door. He made no move to go, but waited for her reply.

'Goodbye — ' she started firmly, and then realised she didn't even know his name. Not that it mattered, she reminded herself quickly. She had no desire to know his name.

'Jack,' he said, filling the gap in her knowledge whether she wanted him to or not. 'Jack Drayton.' He glanced at the delicately boned hand, bare of any ring, that he held in his and frowned. 'You're not really going to marry that pompous idiot?'

'He's not . . . ' Even to discuss Anthony with this man was a betrayal. 'Goodbye, Mr Drayton.' She was very nearly in control of herself now, although it was still extraordinarily difficult to remove her hand from his; not that he made any attempt to hold her, he simply waited for her to make the effort to take her hand away. She finally managed it and he took the weight of the door from her, holding it open, letting in the cold, invigorating blast of street air as if offering her an escape to a more dangerous, more exciting world. His eyes dared her to break loose and although her pulse was beating to his challenge she quickly stepped back as if from the edge of some yawning abyss. She didn't want to escape from the security, the certainty that Anthony represented.

Then, as she was about to turn away and face the inevitable and no doubt deserved dressing down from Anthony, she hesitated. 'You shouldn't be doing this for a living,' she said. 'You have a gift. Use it.' She rushed on. 'There's a jazz club in the city centre. Why don't you try and get a job there?'

His cornflower-blue eyes sparked with amusement. 'Are you prepared to give me a personal reference?'

He was laughing at her now and she lifted her head a little. She knew enough about music to know that he would be welcome anywhere he chose to play. A rather run-down affair like the club in Melchester would welcome him with open arms.

'You don't need any reference from me. If they won't let you in, just stand on the doorstep and play your saxophone, Mr Drayton; it says everything they need to know.' And with that last dangerous slip from reality she made herself turn and walk away from him.

'Nice one, guys,' she quipped, with a flippancy she was far from feeling, and managed a smile for her expectant staff.

'Oh, but — '

'Leave it,' someone snapped, and then she was on the stairs, out of sight and sound of them, leaning against the wall until the weakness passed, until she could gather herself. They could do and say what they liked.

Anthony glanced up as she entered

his office and frowned. 'Has he gone?'

'I saw him off the premises myself,' she assured him, lightly, but that didn't secm to please him very much either. 'I'm sorry about what happened, Anthony,' she said, quickly, hoping that if she made him see that the whole incident had been unimportant he would be able to dismiss it too. 'I'm afraid the girls decided on some fun at my expense. I . . . he . . . rather took me by surprise.'

'Lout,' Anthony muttered. 'But it's a pity you let him kiss you quite so . . . publicly.' She wondered crazily if he would have preferred the scene had taken place in private. A sudden tremor shook her at the thought of being alone with Jack Drayton and, misunderstanding, Anthony was immediately all concern. 'Don't let it upset you, Rosalind. It was a dreadful thing to happen but it's over now. I did warn you when you were made manager of this branch that you had to keep your distance. You're just a little bit too friendly with the staff.'

'I'll bear that in mind,' she said a little stiffly. Her branch had a good atmosphere, and their sales figures were the best in the city, and she was resentful of even such gentle criticism. He seemed to catch her tone and walked around the desk and took her hand, making a determined effort to smile.

'Good. Just a word that that sort of thing isn't acceptable . . . I'll do it for you, if you like.'

'That won't be necessary,' she said, firmly. She had had to fight hard to get this chance as branch manager. She was still new at the job and was constantly aware of Anthony's close eye on her, watching for mistakes. Then she gave herself an internal shake.

His hand was soft, well cared for, as white as her own. She hadn't really noticed before, but Jack Drayton's hand had been hard and tanned and sprinkled with dark hairs. She blotted the comparison from her mind and tried to concentrate on what Anthony was saying.

' . . . seven o'clock.'

'I'm sorry?'

He frowned slightly. 'I said I'll pick you up at seven. I hope you're looking forward to the concert?'

'Oh, yes, very much,' she said, quickly. It was true that she didn't wear Anthony's ring, but it had been understood for a long time that they were to marry when the time was right. It would be madness to throw away such a caring friendship for a moment's passion in a stranger's arms. That unexpected stir of some unknown, almost wanton response to the virility of a bold-eyed man.

She had worked for Nightingale and Drake, Estate Agents and Auctioneers, on Saturdays and in the holidays since she was sixteen. Then her father had left and her mother, holding in the pain, showing nothing, had come close to a breakdown. So at eighteen she had shelved her plans for university and stayed on to become a trainee negotiator. By the time the crisis had passed she knew exactly what she wanted out of life. It certainly didn't include the kind of marriage her mother had endured.

There had always been rows. Rich Parry enjoyed noisy, passionate rows that couldn't be ignored. They had been a feature of her life for as long as she could remember. About his music. Always about late nights at clubs, weekends away. Her mother had never understood his passion for jazz. But then one morning she had left for school and when she came home she had been met by her mother, white-faced, tight-lipped. Her father had abandoned them both, she said. His precious jazz had finally won.

Anthony had been so kind, kept a friendly eye on her work and when they had spent an afternoon together at one of the large riverside houses, taking details, measuring up, they had discovered a mutual interest in music and he had invited her to a concert. Most of her friends had gone away to college and when they came home she found that a gulf had opened up between them. They had seemed so young and irresponsible. Silly almost. Anthony had at least known what she was talking about. So she had gone to the concert and other invitations had followed and the relationship had gradually grown to a point where he had begun to talk quite naturally about 'when we are married'. She was sure that tonight he would want to set the date.

She walked back to her desk and tried to concentrate on her work. It wasn't easy. Piercing blue eyes seemed to dance enticingly before her, and a low voice asked over and over again, 'You're not really going to marry that pompous idiot?' until she wanted to scream. Five-thirty couldn't come soon enough.

Just before that time Anthony appeared in front of her desk. 'I think we'll leave together tonight, Rosalind. As soon as you're ready.'

Knowing that he was only doing this to stop any talk caused by her own rash response to Jack Drayton's kiss, she began to object.

'It's a little early, Anthony . . . '

'Well, it is your birthday,' he said, laughing a little awkwardly. 'I've arranged for someone else to lock up.' She stifled a feeling of irritation as she gathered her belongings and followed him to the side door. He was making far too much of it and she preferred to do her own arranging, but it didn't seem a good idea to argue the point.

It was already dark, a bleak February evening that threatened rain on a freezing wind. As they stood in the doorway a snatch of music carried to them on its icy breath. It was a saxophone played with a searching sweetness that Rosalind instantly recognised, and her heart sank.

They walked slowly down the steps and there on the corner of the square Jack Drayton was sending the blues up to heaven. People paused even in the biting cold to listen for a moment.

'I don't believe it,' Anthony muttered, hurrying her past. 'I won't have it. There must be a by-law against busking here. If he's there in the morning I'm calling the police.' She stared at the tall figure, the street-light shining down on a mane of thick dark hair, throwing his face into hard shadows that hid his expression.

'Anthony, please, leave it. Besides, I don't believe he is busking.' There was no hopeful cap on the ground in front of him. 'He isn't collecting money.'

'Then why is he there? Shall we see just how much it will take to get rid of him?'

Anthony walked over to Jack Drayton and took out his wallet. Rosalind saw him count out some notes and offer them to the man and she groaned with humiliation. How could Anthony do this to her? She stared at the man. How could *he* do this to her? As if aware of her eyes upon him Jack stopped playing and stared back. Their eyes locked momentarily and in that instant she knew why he had stayed.

She didn't wait for the outcome of the interchange between the two men, but fled across the road to the car park, finding a refuge in the little red Metro, parked on the third level, that had come with her promotion to manager. She leaned her forehead against the steering-wheel and took several deep breaths. Some birthday, she thought, and she still had the Shostakovich to get through.

Anthony had a reserved space on the ground floor and by the time she had driven down his sleek blue Daimler was gone. But Jack Drayton had not. He was standing in the exit lane, forcing her to a halt.

Reluctantly she wound down her window. 'Why are you still here?' she demanded. 'Didn't Anthony pay you enough to move on?' It was hateful, but she couldn't help herself.

'There isn't enough money in the world for that, Rosie.' He smiled, relishing the memory. 'I told him he'd better put it back in his piggy bank and save up until he can afford to buy you a ring.'

She stifled a groan. Behind them someone hooted politely. Jack ignored the hint and leaned on the roof of the car, staring down at her. 'Where's he taking you for your birthday treat? A burger bar?'

'A concert and then dinner at Michel's,' she said, a little smugly.

He let out an ironic whistle. 'Just as well I wouldn't take his cash. What concert? The Jay Livingstone Trio are playing at your jazz club, or perhaps that isn't quite his cup of tea?'

She stifled a groan. She had wanted to go. It wasn't often these days that such a group could be tempted into Melchester, but Anthony loathed jazz and she hadn't even dared suggest it. 'It's not *my* jazz club,' she retorted, disappointment lending a sharpness to her voice. 'If you must know, we're going to the Guildhall. The Shostakovich Cello Concerto.'

'Wouldn't you rather come and listen to Jay?' he offered.

'You have tickets?' she asked, surprised. They had not been cheap.

He grinned. 'No need. Jay's an old friend.' He bent down beside her window, examining her face under the lamplight. 'What do you say?'

Her heartbeat began to accelerate again. 'I . . . ' She tore her eyes away from his. 'No. Of course not. Don't be ridiculous.'

'I wasn't being ridiculous, Rosie. You'd much rather come with me. Admit it.'

'I'll admit nothing of the kind.' She put the car into gear and glared at him. Laughing he stood up.

'Better run along, then. You mustn't be late. Perhaps I'll see you later, cheer your soul with a little blues.' He glanced at the instrument case in his hand.

She stared, horrified. 'You wouldn't?'

'Oh, yes,' he said, and his eyes gleamed wickedly in the subdued light. 'I think you know that I would.'

'Haven't you caused enough trouble for one day?' she demanded.

His eyes teased her. 'Rosie, my darling,' he drawled. 'I haven't even begun.' And with that he stepped back, leaving her free to drive away, but she couldn't. Not before he told her why he was tormenting her.

'What do you want from me?' she asked, her wide hazel eyes pleading with him.

'Use your imagination,' he said, roughly.

She gasped then. She wasn't going to use her imagination. It was a dangerous thing, the imagination. It conjured up strong hands and warm kisses to torment her.

'What do you want?' she demanded again. He didn't elaborate, refused to make it easy for her. But she didn't need to be told what he wanted from her. It was there in the raw challenge in his eyes. She felt as if a trap were closing around her. The knowledge that she had sprung it herself offered precious little comfort. She only knew that if she stayed another moment she would lose everything she wanted. Peace, contentment, security. Precious things. All Jack Drayton could offer was momentary passion, a transitory, crazy sort of excitement that would destroy her peace of mind and when it was over, leave nothing but the misery and humiliation her mother had suffered when her father had walked out on them both. She was going to marry Anthony and she didn't know what she was doing even talking to this man.

The person behind had clearly had enough and an impatient horn galvanised her into action. She eased off the handbrake and put her foot down on the accelerator. The car shot forward and abruptly stalled. She grabbed at the ignition key, but the car wouldn't start and the irritation from behind had suddenly become a chorus of people eager to get home. 'Idiot!' she said, furious with herself. Why on earth had she even spoken to the man. She was going to be late and Anthony hated to be kept waiting. There were tears pricking at her eyelids when the door opened beside her.

He took one look at her face and swore volubly, then put an ice-cold hand on hers, stopping the desperate churning of the engine. 'Move over, Rosie. You're in no fit state to drive,' he said, very gently.

'And who's fault is that?' she demanded, angrily.

'That's open to debate. You didn't have to stop.' He threw the saxophone on to the back seat and waited and, conscious of the queue of cars behind her, she moved over. He pushed the driving seat back as far as it would go and climbed in beside her. The car started at the first touch. Everything would start at his touch, she thought, hopelessly. Even her. Especially her.

'Why *did* you stop, Rosie?' he asked, as he wove the little car through the evening rush hour with almost reckless panache and the traffic seemed to melt before him.

'I should have run you over?' she asked, angrily.

'Is that the only reason?' They were paused at the lights and he turned to her. His brilliant eyes locked with her dark ones and the bone-jolting shock of an electric current seemed to shoot through her. It was a moment of pure terror in which the orderly fabric of her life came under threat. She tore her eyes away from his and stared ahead blindly, not seeing the cars, or the lights, or the shops.

'Anthony said he would call the police to have you moved on if you were outside the office tomorrow,' she said, her voice sounding odd even in her own ears. 'Not that you will be,' she added a little fiercely. 'You'll have caught your death of cold by then.'

'And that would worry you? I'm flattered. But it's pneumonia you get from standing out in the cold and rain. Where shall I park?'

'What?'

'You'd better come back down to earth before your precious Anthony sets eyes on you, Rosie. According to your instructions, this is where you live. Where do you normally park?'

She stared blindly at the old house long ago converted into small flats, barely recognising that she was home. 'There,' she said, miserably, indicating a spot in front of the figure four neatly painted on the wall. He pulled up and for a moment they both sat in silence.

Then Rosalind lifted her head to stare at the hard profile of this man who had come from nowhere and seemed determined to overturn her life.

'Why did you kiss me like that, Jack?' she asked. 'Was it included in the price?'

He didn't look at her. His eyes were fixed on some point in the distance, his hands gripping the steering-wheel. 'You can't pay for a kiss like that, Rosalind Parry. That kind of flashpoint only happens between two people once in a lifetime.'

'What kind?' As he turned to face her, she knew she shouldn't have asked.

'It's a kind of recognition. But you know what happened, Rosie,' he said. 'You kissed me back. Remember?' She didn't want to remember. It was important that she didn't remember. His face was like stone in the colour-draining street light. 'Don't kid yourself that what happened today is something you can ignore. The memory of it will torment you. You'll never be happy married to Anthony Harlowe.'

A small croak of anguish escaped her lips. 'You don't know what you're talking about,' she hurled at him defiantly. 'I love Anthony.'

A small fierce sound escaped his lips.

'Him? Or his money?' His mouth was a hard line.

She stared at him in disbelief. 'It's got nothing to do with his money.'

'No? Keep saying it, Rosie. You might get to believe it.' He didn't wait for her furious response, but climbed out of the car, opened the door for her, locked up and handed her the keys. She didn't move and he said, a little sharply, 'Better hurry. I don't think you should risk upsetting Harlowe twice in one day, do you? He didn't appear to have much sense of humour.'

She knew she would never be ready on time but, even so, still found it impossible to tear herself away. 'What will you do? How will you get home?' she asked.

'Still worrying about me?'

'I don't want to,' she said, a little desperately. 'But I can't seem to help it. I feel . . . responsible.'

He briefly touched her cold cheek. 'You are responsible. It will make me feel good to know that you're worrying about me walking all the way back to town.' He put out a hand and looked up at the sky. 'I think it's about to rain in earnest.'

A heavy raindrop splashed on to her face and she stared upwards into the black night and raged against the elements. 'No!'

Jack Drayton laughed with a flash of white teeth in the lamplight and turned up the collar of his denim jacket. 'That's right, Rosie. Worry about me getting soaked to the skin. Think about the rain running down my face, dripping down the back of my neck. Cold February rain. And when you're warm in your expensive French restaurant with Anthony Harlowe and afterwards, when he's holding you close and kissing you, remember this: we'll both know that it will be me that's on your mind.' He turned from her and strode away on long legs, back towards the town centre.

2

'Jack!' Rosalind called desperately after him, then impulsively took a few steps after him. 'Jack, please!'

He stopped and turned. 'Please what, Rosie?' he asked, softly.

'There's no need to get wet. Take my car.' She took another step towards him, holding out the keys and he glanced at them briefly before raising his eyes once more to meet hers. But he made no move to meet her halfway. He simply bared his teeth in a smile.

'That's a rash offer, Rosie,' he warned. Confusion brought a dark flush to her cheeks. Rash? That was putting it mildly. What on earth was she thinking of? She was behaving like an idiot, almost . . . almost, as if she wanted to make certain she would see him again. Her hand snapped shut over the keys. That was ridiculous. Nothing could be further from the truth and she was about to make that quite clear, but he swiftly covered the ground between them and before she could speak had captured her chin and raised her face to his. 'You can't get me off your conscience that easily, Rosie. It's you I want, not your car. You know that.' He brushed her lips with his. Hardly a kiss. A promise. 'Enjoy yourself tonight . . . if you can. Perhaps I'll see you later.'

Before she could protest, tell this infuriating man that she never wanted to set eyes on him, ever again, he had released her and was striding purposefully away.

Rosalind Parry felt an almost overwhelming urge to stamp on the pavement. But she had long ago learned to keep her temper under tight control so she contented herself with glaring after the dark figure responsible for this sudden desire to let rip. He was rapidly disappearing into the gloomy night and she raised her voice to call after him. 'I won't worry about you, Jack Drayton,' she called defiantly. 'Not for one minute. I hope you do get pneumonia.' As the rain began to splash against her face hot tears stung at her eyelids. 'I will enjoy myself tonight.' The sound of his laughter filtered back through the darkness. 'I will,' she repeated with determination. 'You just see.'

Then she fled to the second-floor flat she shared with a friend from her schooldays. Sarah was late home from work which was just as well. She was too perceptive by half and Rosalind was relieved that she would have privacy in which to re-order her overwrought emotions.

Not that she had much time to spare for such self-indulgence. She glanced at the clock and with a tiny shriek of anguish dived for the bathroom. A quick shower, a little make-up. She sprayed herself with the scent Sarah had bought for her birthday and immediately wished she hadn't. The fragrance was heavy, seductive, not her type of thing. But it was too late to do anything about it. She brushed out her dark copper hair. Free of constraining pins, it bounced back into an irresistible curl that framed her face. Another quick glance at the clock confirmed that she didn't have time to put it up properly and experience had taught her that it would fight its way free of any half-hearted attempt at the job. As if to confirm this fact the doorbell rang. Seven o'clock precisely. Anthony was never late. He was never early, either. She caught herself up. What on earth had made her think that? As if somehow predictability was a fault. It was this very predictability that made Anthony so precious.

She fastened the last button of her black velvet evening suit and raised her hand to the scooped neckline with its satin-bound collar, suddenly realising just how low it was cut. In the boutique, against the flamboyant low-cut evening dresses, it had seemed positively demure. Now she saw her mistake. The fitted jacket emphasised her figure, the slightly flared skirt displayed rather more of her long legs than she had realised and she wondered uneasily if Anthony would quite like it, but it was too late to change so, with a last, slightly dismayed glance at her reflection, she went to open the door.

In the mad rush to get ready she hadn't had a single moment to worry about Jack Drayton, but the raindrops clinging to Anthony's soft brown hair were an instant reminder that outside it was cold and wet and very uninviting and her mind's eye immediately flashed up a picture of him, soaking wet, walking the long cold miles back into the town centre.

She immediately banished it, telling herself firmly that it was his own fault if he was wet. She hadn't asked him to kiss her, and her fingers flew to her lips as if to brush away the memory. 'I'll get my coat,' she said, quickly, turning away, ashamed of the feelings his lips had evoked.

But Anthony stopped her. 'We have a moment, Rosalind. I haven't given you your birthday present.' The package he took from his pocket was small. 'Happy birthday,' he said and kissed her cheek. Rosalind held the beautifully wrapped package, anguished with guilt that she could be so distracted by an easy smile and a careless kiss. 'Well? Aren't you going to open it?' he prompted.

She tore at the gold paper and uncovered a jeweller's box. On the dark blue velvet nestled a tiny gold watch. 'Oh! It's lovely, Anthony. Thank you.' She leaned forward and kissed his mouth, an unexpectedly warm gesture that took him by surprise. She had never taken the initiative in their rather restrained lovemaking. But right now she was so confused about the way she had reacted to Jack that she felt the need to convince them both that she loved him. She wanted him to take her in his arms and make her forget what had happened.

Instead he took the watch from her

hand. 'I'll fasten it for you, shall I?' he asked. Then he frowned. 'What's the matter? Don't you like it?'

'It's lovely, Anthony. I said so.'

'Then you sighed,' he said, a little edgily.

'Did I?' she asked, the slightest frown creasing the wide forehead. It was true that for a moment she had wanted Anthony to kiss her, drive away the buried Cinderella dream of every girl. The dream of the perfect lover riding out of the mists to claim her. Lancelot. The Young Lochinvar. Romance. Foolishness. Jack Drayton was no Prince Charming. On the contrary, he was the kind of man careful mothers warned their daughters about. Not that she had needed warning. She had the example of her father as warning enough.

Her partnership with Anthony would be something built on trust, mutual interest, friendship. Not some passionate flight of fancy. She had seen the misery that sort of relationship could cause when it fell apart at first hand.

Yet, as he fastened his expensive gift in place, she found herself wondering a little shakily what it would be like to share a bed with Anthony, what their wedding-night would be like. She stared at the top of his head as he bent over her wrist. Would he undress her, she wondered, touch her body, make love to her with care and tenderness? Or would he disappear into the bathroom and return respectably clad in pyjamas, expecting her to be waiting for him under the covers with the light off. She lifted her fingers to her lips as her subconscious jolted her with the memory of the taste of Jack Drayton's mouth on hers and she knew at that moment exactly what it would be like to be loved by him. No time for thought. Only sensation. Shattering, intense sensation.

She jerked edgily from his touch. 'We'd better go,' she said, turning away to hide the sudden betraying heat that seared her cheeks at such shocking thoughts. 'We'll be late.'

'There's a while yet. I left plenty of

time. Aren't you going to put up your hair?'

She caught a glance of herself in the mirror. She only wore her spectacles for close work and now her hazel eyes appeared huge and mysterious in her delicately boned face. Her hair, a calmer tone than the fiery Celtic copper red of her father, the colour of a chestnut brand new from its shell, framed her face in a mass of curls. She looked different tonight. Like her hair, not quite under control.

'It will take too long.' Then, because she had sounded a little fierce, she forced a smile. 'You don't mind, do you?'

'It makes you look rather young,' he objected.

She took his arm. 'Don't be silly, Anthony.' He looked slightly taken aback at her words and she wondered if anyone had ever called him silly before. She had to fight down the totally unexpected desire to giggle. But it had been a day full of unexpected emotions.

'I'm twenty-four today. Positively ancient,' she quickly added to placate him, and it was a relief to see an answering smile lift his mouth.

Two hours of Shostakovich certainly cured her of any desire to giggle. For a while she tried to concentrate, but she found the music difficult and in the end she stopped trying to follow it, letting it wash over her. But inside her head a very different kind of music began to improvise long sliding scales on a tenor saxophone. She closed her eyes and saw a pair of strong hands moving surely over the keys, the street light gleaming on burnished metal and black hair that curled on to a denim collar.

'Rosalind?' She opened her eyes to the enthusiastic applause of the audience and quickly joined in, but Anthony leaned closer and murmured. 'Are you feeling well?'

'Just a slight headache. I closed my eyes. I'm afraid I may have dropped off for a moment.'

He looked at her with concern. 'I

expect you're hungry. I don't suppose for a moment you had time to eat anything when you got home.' Unlike Anthony, whose mother would undoubtedly have been waiting with tea and sandwiches. She wondered briefly what he would do without his mother to administer to every need. She found Mrs Harlowe's slavish devotion to Anthony's every whim a little hard to take. Her father, for all his faults, had loved to cook and had never expected to be waited on. Some of her happiest childhood memories were of the time they had spent together in the kitchen preparing his favourite recipes conspiring to surprise her mother. They had been so close. She had trusted him so completely. The thought jabbed at the painful memory of his desertion and she retreated from it, back to the present. To Anthony.

Maybe he would suggest his mother should live with them when they were married. That would solve everything. Maybe, she thought, he would simply suggest she move in with the two of them. The traitorous thought jarred into her head and she quickly excused herself to reclaim her coat, afraid that he would read it on her face. She didn't dislike Anthony's mother, just thought she was rather silly, but living under the same roof might impose more strain on their relationship than it could easily take. Anthony was marrying a career woman and he would simply have to learn to be a little more self-reliant.

But he was right, of course. She hadn't even had time for a cup of tea when she'd got home. Not that she felt particularly hungry, and the headache that she had invented a moment ago was threatening to become a reality.

The fresh air was a momentary reprieve, but as they got closer to the restaurant and the growing certainty that Jack Drayton would be there to embarrass her further she began to feel sick. She pressed her fingers to her temple.

'Is your headache worse?' Anthony asked. 'You haven't looked yourself all evening and I think I can guess why,' he added, his voice heavy with meaning.

'It's been a bit hectic at work, that's all.'

'I know you've been busy.' He leaned across and patted her hand. 'You've really done very well. Proved your point,' he conceded, somewhat magnanimously. He had made no secret of his opinion that he thought she was too young for such responsibility but had been overruled by the senior partners. 'But soon you'll be able to take things more easily. I believe it's time to set a date for the wedding. We won't wait too long.'

The surge of happiness that she had anticipated at this moment did not materialise. Instead her head began to throb painfully.

They had arrived at Michel's and Anthony dropped her by the entrance before parking. Rosalind glanced quickly around but there was no sign of Jack Drayton. She knew she should have felt relieved. But it was only the relief of having put off a visit to the dentist. She had the unhappy feeling that he wasn't the kind of man to give up on something he wanted. And he wanted her. He had said so. His eyes had told her so.

They were shown to their seats and uncharacteristically Anthony immediately ordered a bottle of champagne.

'Anthony, no.' The combination of a headache and champagne would be disaster. But he seemed determinedly merry.

'It's a special occasion, after all,' he insisted.

'Well, just a sip,' she conceded. 'It's a long time since I've eaten.'

'As you wish,' he said, finally becoming irritated, and she left it. The evening seemed to be progressing steadily downhill. No. It wasn't just the evening. It had started this afternoon when Jack Drayton had burst into her life. It was all his fault. ' . . . Mother to look after you.' She forced herself to concentrate on what Anthony was saying. 'No more rushing about when we're married, Rosalind. You'll be a lady of leisure. She was saying tonight how much she's looking forward to it. You'll be able to go on shopping trips together.'

'Who?'

'Mother and you.' He looked at her coldly. 'I don't believe you've been listening to a word I was saying,' he remonstrated.

'Yes. Yes I have. But I've no wish to be a lady of leisure,' she said, quietly. 'I like my job.' She chose not to comment on the pleasures of shopping with Mrs Harlowe. She had done it once, taken her into the city centre to buy a hat. She hoped never to have to repeat the experience.

'Of course you do. It's just . . . surely you won't want to carry on, not once we're married?' He sounded slightly shocked.

'Why not?' She wondered why it had never occurred to her that Anthony would expect her to stay at home all day and become simply Mrs Harlowe. The champagne arrived, diverting his attention, and the waiter opened the bottle and poured two glasses.

Anthony picked them up and handed one to her. 'I think we've waited long enough, Rosalind. I told Mother we would set the date for the wedding tonight.' Rosalind sipped the champagne to moisten lips that were suddenly dry. 'I thought the first week in May,' he said.

'May?'

He frowned. 'Is there something wrong with that?'

'An old aunt of my mother's always said May was unlucky for weddings. My mother was married in May.' She made an effort to pull herself together. 'Superstitious nonsense, of course.' The waiter refilled their glasses.

'The first is a Saturday.'

She managed a smile. 'Lovely. I'll let Mr Nightingale know that I'll want some time off.' She rubbed her forehead. 'It's so hot in here.'

'Leave all the arrangements with me,' Anthony said, picking up the menu. 'I'll organise everything.'

'If you like. But May doesn't give us much time to find somewhere to live . . .' Her head seemed to be drifting off somewhere by itself. 'Although there is a lovely village house just come on the books; it has the most beautiful garden . . .'

He looked puzzled. 'There's no need to worry about househunting, Rosalind. My house is big enough for the three of us.'

'Three . . . ?' She giggled. 'Three's a crowd . . .' She looked at her glass. It was empty. She was just so dry. 'Do you think I could have some water?'

Anthony frowned and summoned a waiter. 'You don't have to worry about Mother. She's delighted to have you live with us. It's such a relief that you two get on so well. She suggested that you come round at the weekend and sort out the rooms with her.' He looked up when she didn't answer. 'I know you'll be tactful. It's been her home for a very long time.'

She knew she should make some sort of stand. 'Anthony — '

He raised his head from the menu. 'Have you decided what you want to eat?'

The protest died on her lips. 'Not yet.' She bent her head over the enormous menu but found it hard to concentrate on food. Half an hour ago she had been treating the idea as a joke and now she had been presented with a *fait accompli*. Rosalind thought about the big square house in the well-groomed middle-class suburbs of Melchester. She reached for her glass but it was empty. Anthony refilled it and she sipped absently. Of course it would be far too big for Mrs Harlowe to live in on her own. But all her friends were in the neighbourhood and Rosalind could see she wouldn't want to move away to something smaller. And she would be at work all day. She pushed the thought of the beautiful stone house in Wickham firmly out of her mind and concentrated on the menu. After all, what time did she have for gardening?

'Rosalind? Are you all right?' Anthony half stood as she rose abruptly from her seat.

'Excuse me, Anthony.' She dived for the cloakroom and was promptly sick. She sat quivering and slicked with sweat. The attendant wiped her face with a damp tissue and waved a bottle of smelling salts under her nose. It helped, but there was no way she could face the restaurant. She sent a message for Anthony to meet her in the entrance.

When Anthony appeared he actually looked quite angry. 'What's the matter, Rosalind?' Then he saw how white she was and without another word went for the car.

He drove her home in silence, for which she was grateful and saw her safely inside.

'Perhaps it's the flu,' he said, awkwardly. 'There seems to be a lot of it about.'

'Perhaps,' she agreed, unwilling to expose her own stupidity at drinking two glasses of champagne on an empty stomach. Or was it three? It didn't matter. She had known one would be too many. 'Would you like some coffee?' she offered, automatically.

'No, I'll let you get straight to bed. I expect you'll feel a lot better for a good night's sleep.' He dropped a kiss on her forehead.

'Yes. I'll see you in the morning.'

'Perhaps you should take the day off.'

'I'll be fine in the morning. Really,' she assured him when he seemed to hesitate.

She stood there for a moment, listening to the sound of his footsteps retreating, then closed the door with a sigh and went into the empty flat.

She put on the kettle to make a hot drink and went to change into her nightdress. Anthony was right about one thing. She was tired, but she had the unhappy feeling that a good night's sleep would not be so easy to come by.

Too much had happened for one day. Except it hadn't been the decision about the wedding that had sent her thoughts into a spin. It had been the encounter with Jack Drayton. And that was all wrong. She knew it.

As Rose made the tea, she smiled somewhat ironically. Despite Jack's firm conviction to the contrary, she congratulated herself, she had not worried about him all evening. Not for one minute. She wondered why he had decided not to come to Michel's. Not that it mattered. She was just grateful that he hadn't turned up. Grateful too that he hadn't accepted her crazy offer to lend him her car. She would never see the wretched man again and that was just fine with her.

She curled up in front of the gas fire. Anthony was right. He was always right. She was tired and although they hadn't had the chance to discuss where they might go for their honeymoon she allowed herself to dwell on the prospect. Somewhere warm, she thought.

The south of France. Spain. Portugal. Capri, perhaps. Spring was a glorious time of year for the warmer parts of the Mediterranean. She would pick up some brochures in her lunch break tomorrow and perhaps they could decide at the weekend.

Sarah came home a little after twelve and was surprised to find Rosalind dozing in front of the fire. 'I thought you would still be out celebrating with the big man.' She checked her watch. 'Or is it past his bedtime?'

Sarah's constant reference to Anthony as the 'big man' irritated Rosalind. It was true that he was barely an inch taller than her, but she was five foot nine in her stockinged feet and that wasn't exactly short. And Sarah was always asking when he was going to 'stop over', speculating on what he would look like over the breakfast table before he had got his hair under control. In fact she was well aware that Sarah did not like Anthony very much at all. The feeling was mutual.

'I had a headache. We came home early.'

'I bet he was really disappointed.'

'Sarah!'

Her friend was immediately contrite. 'Sorry, Rose. But he wasn't very keen, was he?' She pulled a sombre face and did a very passable imitation of Anthony at his most pompous. 'French food is not exactly my cup of tea, Rosalind, but if it's what you want . . .' She hesitated. 'He does rather like to have things his own way.'

'We all like to get our own way, Sarah,' Rosalind said, pushing back the uncomfortable thought that sometimes he never even considered that anyone else might have a viewpoint at all. She held out her hand and displayed her new watch. 'He bought me this for my birthday.'

Sarah bent to look at it. 'He's not cheap, I'll give him that. I wonder if he'll break into his piggy bank and buy you a ring now?' She saw Rosalind's shocked expression and, completely misunderstanding, threw her arms around her friend. 'I'm sorry, Rose, that was a beastly thing to say. I know you're not marrying him for his money.'

'No. I'm not marrying him for his money.' It was just that Jack had said the same thing and the words brought him sharply into focus.

Sarah hesitated. 'Which only leaves one vital question — why are you going to marry him, Rose?'

'Because I want to. I'm very fond of him,' Rosalind replied, stiffly, conscious that Sarah was again echoing Jack's question.

'Fond?' Sarah let out an exasperated little noise that expressed her feelings precisely. 'I'm fond of my mother's prize Tamworth pig,' she declared. 'Marriage requires a little more than that, wouldn't you say? I don't understand you, Rose. You're young, quite stunning to look at when you don't dress in those dowdy things that Anthony likes. He's turning you into a middle-aged woman before you've had time to grow up properly. Dump him, Rose. There's a whole world of real men out there — '

'Anthony is a real man,' she said fervently. 'He's kind. He's reliable — '

'Admirable qualities, Rose, but are they enough? I know you have to kiss a lot of frogs before you find the prince ... but to keep kissing the same frog — '

'And how was your Prince Charming this evening?' Rose interrupted.

Sarah took one look at Rosalind's face and stopped. They had known one another a long time and she recognised the danger signs: the whiteness around the mouth, a certain spark that turned her eyes very green. There had been a time when Rosalind's temper had made life very lively at school. She wondered briefly if Anthony had ever seen her friend in full flood. She very much doubted it and she wondered how long it would be before he found out he had married a spitfire. Rosalind had battled to control her temper, but Sarah suspected that married life with Anthony might strain that control to breaking point. She envied the lucky fly on the wall who witnessed the resulting mayhem, but kept that thought to herself.

'I'm sorry, Rose. It's really none of my business. Forget I said anything. Please.'

'It's forgotten,' she said, a little stiffly. 'We've set the date for the wedding. The first of May. I was going to ask you to be my bridesmaid, or whatever it is brides have in register offices. Of course, if you'd rather not — '

'A register office wedding? Surely your mother will expect a church wedding, with hundreds of relations, white dress, choir, the lot. You certainly deserve the white dress and not many of us can say that.'

'I haven't got hundreds of relations and we all deserve a white dress, Sarah. It's an attitude of mind. A promise of forever,' she added, fiercely. 'It doesn't matter where you say the words. Will you stand with me?'

Sarah sighed. 'If you're sure it's what you really want?'

Rosalind nodded firmly, pushing away the image that Sarah had conjured up of the old grey stone church where she had been baptised and had gone with her mother every Sunday throughout her childhood. Her father too, on the rare occasions that he hadn't been away playing at some gig. But if she had a church wedding her mother would insist on paying for it. This way she could keep it small, informal and she would pay for it herself.

'Yes, Sarah,' she said firmly. 'It's exactly what I want.'

The other girl hesitated for a moment, then said, 'In that case we'd better start looking for something to wear. What about Saturday?'

'I have to visit Mrs Harlowe on Saturday. I was thinking of taking a day off one day next week and going up to London. Can you manage that?'

'I'm not sure,' Sarah said, yawning.

'I'll have to let you know. Well, I'm to my bed. *I'm* not marrying my boss so I'll have to be up bright and early in the morning.'

Rosalind followed suit and immediately fell asleep, but her dreams were nightmarish. Anthony was there, wearing a pair of striped pyjamas. He kept appearing to check the time on her watch and warn her she must come to bed, apparently oblivious of the fact that Jack Drayton, dripping with rain, was gradually undressing her. Anthony was supposed to protect her. She wanted him to protect her, keep her safe, but he didn't. She woke in the dark, sweating, her heart pounding. It was nearly six and she threw off the covers and went to have a bath.

By the time she made a stab at breakfast and applied rather more make-up than usual, she was ready to face the day. Her hair firmly twisted into a neat chignon, her favourite tan Chanel-style suit and a simple cream blouse completed the picture, and if her limbs felt leaden, she at least looked the part of an elegant young business-woman.

It had stopped raining at last and as she unlocked her car, the sun was trying to break through the cloud cover with a promise that things were back on an even keel. She got into the car, turned the ignition and reached for the clutch. Her foot didn't quite reach it.

Rosalind frowned, for a moment unable to understand what had happened. Then she knew. Jack Drayton had pushed the seat back and found a way to push himself back into her consciousness just when she thought she had him firmly stowed away in her mind's attic with the rest of life's unwanted debris. She slid the seat forward and very firmly turned her mind to the day ahead. He was yesterday. What happened to him was none of her concern. She was going to marry Anthony she thought, a little fiercely. Soon. And she put the car into gear and drove to an early appointment with a potential client who was thinking of letting her flat.

She hung up her coat and walked across to her desk where she found a square white envelope with her name on it on top of the post. She ripped it open and took out the card. The handwriting was bold and to the point. Like the man. Like the message. 'Don't forget our lunch date, Rosie. Twelve-thirty at the wine bar. Jack.'

How dared he believe for one moment she would go to the wine bar with him? Besides, she had other plans for her lunch hour. She tore the card in two and dropped it in the bin.

'What was that?' Anthony's approach had been silent and his voice made her jump guiltily.

'Nothing. Junk mail,' she said, with some feeling.

He looked at her closely. 'Mmm. How are you this morning? Should you have come in? You still look rather pale.'

'Fine, really,' she said, reassuringly, trying to ignore the trembling that seemed to suddenly affect her legs.

He nodded, apparently satisfied. 'I'm going to be busy for the next couple of days, but I'll see you on Saturday when you come over to see Mother. We can talk over the wedding arrangements then.'

'I'll have to let Mum know what the arrangements are in plenty of time. I think we should keep it simple.'

'There's no need to bother your mother. We'll have the wedding at home.' He waited for her agreement. 'If you've no objection,' he added, quickly, when she didn't immediately respond.

'I'll speak to her. See what she would like.'

'Your mother is an amazing woman, Rosalind. The way she picked herself up after your father left her . . . '

'She had no choice, Anthony,' she said, with feeling. 'There was no one else to do it for her.'

'Quite. But she doesn't have much time these days. I think you should leave it all to my mother. She's used to entertaining.' He cleared his throat. 'Well, I must go, or I'll be late. We can talk about this on Saturday. I'll pick you up at about three.'

'There's no need,' she said, edgily. 'I'll drive myself.' Then, relenting because she knew he meant to be kind, 'I have quite a few appointments on Saturday and I don't know when I'll get away. It will be simpler if I come when I can,' she added, gently.

He glanced at his watch. 'Right. I'll see you some time Saturday afternoon, then. Goodbye, Rosalind.'

'Goodbye, Anthony.' But he was already halfway across the office. She sat down at her desk. Sometimes, she thought, fiercely, just once in a while, I wish he'd forget to be so damned *formal*. What was the matter with a kiss? They were getting married, for heaven's sake. It wasn't going to shock anyone. Even Mr Nightingale, the senior partner, kissed his wife when she came into the office. Maybe when

Anthony was a full partner and her hair was a little grey, he would kiss her when she dropped by at the office after doing some shopping. She caught her breath. Something crazy was happening to her, something she didn't understand. Until yesterday she and Anthony had been in perfect accord about everything. Suddenly she was finding fault in everything he did. She picked up an envelope and tore it open. Pre-wedding nerves. That must be it.

She began to work through the pile of mail and the morning flew by. She despatched one of the negotiators to take instructions for two new properties, arranged to meet someone for a viewing for the property in Wickham for Saturday morning and went down to the newspaper office to check the advertisement in the weekend property feature.

When she returned there was a list of messages to keep her busy until lunchtime.

'I'm getting a sandwich, Rosalind.

Do you want anything?'

She raised her head from a set of details she was checking and smiled. 'You fuss over me more than my mother, Julie. I'll have beef and coleslaw on brown bread.'

'I'll bring you a yoghurt as well. You don't eat enough.'

She gave in gracefully. Her secretary was only a few years older than Rosalind, but she clucked over her like a mother hen. 'Good idea.' She paused. 'I don't suppose you're going anywhere near the travel agent?'

'It wouldn't be any trouble. What do you want?'

'Just a few brochures. Nothing exotic.' The phone rang and she reached automatically for it, then realising the time she wondered uneasily if it were Jack. She hadn't met him in the wine bar and she wouldn't put it past him to ring and jog her memory. She withdrew her hand. 'Could you answer that for me?'

Julie grinned. 'Who are you avoiding?'

'Just see who it is.'

She picked up the phone and answered, then held it out to Rosalind and whispered conspiratorially, 'It's your . . . young man.' She handed Rosalind the phone and went to lunch.

Rosalind looked at the phone as if it might bite, then unhappily put the receiver to her ear. 'Yes?'

'Rosalind?'

'Oh, Anthony, what can I do for you?' Her heart rate gradually resumed its normal steady pace.

'Nothing. It's just that I've been asked to a golf tournament on Saturday afternoon. I've told Mother and she said to let you know that she's expecting you anyway and that you must stay for dinner. You'll be company for one another and you won't have anything else to do, will you?'

Rosalind had no special wish to spend the evening alone with Mrs Harlowe. An afternoon fencing around the subject of their living arrangements would be quite enough. She heard the bell ring as someone came into the office and raised her eyes above the glass panelling that separated her from the front office to check that there was someone available to deal with any query.

But it wasn't someone looking for a house. Jack Drayton was rapidly approaching her corner, determination written on every feature. 'I'll phone her this evening, Anthony,' she said, quickly. 'Right now I have a lunch appointment.' And she hung up before Anthony could ask who it was with.

3

'Hello, Rosie.'

She glared at him. 'Don't call me that,' she said, crossly. Her father had always called her Rosie and she had no wish to be reminded of him.

'What do you prefer? Miss Parry? Rose? Or shall I call you *Rosalind* in that possessive tone that Harlowe uses?'

'I would prefer it if you just stayed away altogether,' she said, but her heart leapt dangerously as he smiled at her. 'Go away, Jack Drayton.'

'You know you don't mean it, Rosie. I distinctly heard you tell someone that you have a lunch date and if you stand me up now that will make a liar out of you. Besides, you have to eat.' He firmly grasped her elbow, lifted her from her chair and ignoring her protest, steered her towards the door in a manner that brooked no dispute.

They passed Julie on the way out. 'Are you going out, Rosalind?' she asked, surprised. 'What about these?' She held the bag containing Rosalind's lunch and the travel brochures.

Jack relieved Julie of them before Rosalind could intervene. 'Hold Miss Parry's calls,' he instructed her. 'She's coming out to lunch with me.'

Julie threw a startled look at Rosalind. 'In that case you won't want this.' She retrieved the sandwich. 'What shall I tell Mr Harlowe if he phones?' she asked, a touch of disapproval in her voice.

'I'm sure you'll think of something,' Jack said, with a smile.

'For goodness' sake don't encourage her,' Rosalind muttered as he led her down the steps, cross at the way she was allowing herself to be manipulated. 'I'm beginning to think Anthony was right. It's time I was a little firmer with these girls.' She stopped and turned to him. 'And with you,' she added.

'Oh, I'm a hopeless case,' he

responded, firmly moving her on. 'And there's nothing wrong with your staff. Perhaps you should just try being a little less tough on yourself, Rosie.'

'I told you not to call me that,' she protested, trying to shake him off. Then as someone passing turned to look at them she lowered her voice and hissed, 'Why don't you leave me alone?'

'Because when I make a date, Rosie my love, I expect it to be kept.'

'I'm not your 'love', and we don't have a date. You've got a nerve coming back to the office. If Anthony had been there — '

'But he wasn't. And where you're concerned, Miss Parry, I have all the nerve it takes.' His expression dared her to contradict him. 'Stand me up again and you'll find out exactly what I'm capable of.'

She stopped and stared at him. The situation was getting out of hand. 'What?' she demanded, lifting her head and challenging him. 'What will you do?'

'You could always try me and find

out, Rosie. If you dare?'

'There isn't going to be a next time!'

He released her arm and opened the wine bar door. 'After you.'

'This is ridiculous.'

'I agree, we're letting the cold air inside. In you go.'

'No . . . ' But her reluctance was edged with a tingle of excitement. Protest she might, but she found Jack Drayton an invigorating enigma and she wanted to know more about him. He was a brilliant musician, down on his luck perhaps, doing what he could to make a little money. It was possible she could help him. She still sometimes saw people her father had played with. If she asked one of them to listen to him . . . Having convinced herself she was only having lunch with Jack in order to help him, Rosalind Parry stopped fighting the inevitable and stepped into the warm atmosphere of the wine bar.

'What would you like to drink?' he asked.

'A fruit juice, please,' she said,

primly. Then, because he smiled a little, she added, 'I'm driving.'

'Of course.' He took the holiday brochures from her hands and held a chair out for her at one of the small tables tucked away in the corner.

'Couldn't we sit at the bar? I can't stay long.'

'You'll stay just as long as I want you to, Rosie,' he said, easily. 'After all, you've nothing to be afraid of. You've told me that you are safely attached to the well-heeled Mr Harlowe. How can I be such a threat to your peace of mind?'

'You're not!' she retorted. 'And I'm not afraid of you. I just want you to leave me alone.'

'Keep saying it and you might actually get to believe it,' he suggested with a casual insolence that caught her breath in her throat. 'Any particular fruit juice, or do you feel reckless enough to let me choose?'

'Orange!' she snapped, then coloured at her rudeness. 'Please,' she added, quickly.

'Orange it is,' he affirmed, with that infuriating, knowing smile and made for the bar where he flirted outrageously with the fair-haired girl who served him. They were laughing and she suddenly felt a stab of something very much like jealousy, like someone abandoned by her boyfriend at a party for a more beguiling companion. She turned quickly away. Who he flirted with was none of her business. In fact she should be grateful that it wasn't her. She *was* grateful, she told herself, and picked up one of her holiday books and began to flip through the pages, although she couldn't have said what was on the colourful pages.

'Planning a holiday?' Jack asked, as he put her drink on the table. He too was drinking fruit juice she noticed with surprise.

'A honeymoon, actually,' she said, with some satisfaction. His mouth tightened slightly as he sat down and reached for her hand.

'But still no ring?' He shrugged. 'Well,

he was warned. On his own head be it.'

'For your information we set the date for the wedding last night. The first Saturday in May.' She wanted to pull away from the warm touch of his fingers, but he wouldn't let her.

He fastened his eyes on her. 'Come on, Rosie. You're not really going to marry that stuffed shirt? Money isn't everything.'

'It helps,' she said, rising to the lure, and could have bitten off her tongue for being so stupid. It hurt that he could think her so shallow, but it was too late to deny the accusation. Besides, she had no need to justify herself to this man. It didn't matter in the least what he thought of her. 'I am going to marry Anthony,' she said, stonily. 'I don't make promises that I'm not prepared to keep.' She shifted uncomfortably under his cynical scrutiny. 'What happened to you last night, anyway?' she asked, in an attempt to change the subject. 'I was expecting to be serenaded outside Michel's.'

'You missed me?' His eyes seemed to seek the far corners of her mind. 'Then I'm sorry I didn't come, but if you'd bothered to look in the back of your car, Rosie, you'd know that I left the sax there. I called round this morning to pick it up, but your car had gone. Do you normally go to work so early?' He was very still, his gaze watchful. 'Or perhaps you just hadn't come home from your exciting night out?'

Her eyes flashed furiously. 'How dare you!'

The corners of his mouth creased into a smile of satisfaction and finally he released her hand. 'An interesting response, Rosie. Very revealing. Now, let's see if I can help with the honeymoon. I always rather fancied the Indian Ocean myself. Sand, sea and — er — coconuts. What do you think?'

She ignored him, furious with herself for falling into his trap.

'I came home early because I had a headache,' she said.

'I wonder why? Too much Shostakovich?

Or too much Anthony Harlowe?' He clearly didn't expect an answer because he immediately returned his attention to the travel brochure. 'Well, Rosie?' he prompted. 'Where's it to be?'

'I told you not to call me that!'

'You're just avoiding the question, Rosie,' he persisted and the word grated over her skin.

She turned abruptly from his searching eyes. 'You're impossible!'

'No, I'm not,' he said, adopting a hurt expression that didn't fool her for a minute. 'In fact I'm generally regarded to be a very reasonable sort of man. But I can see you're not very eager to discuss your honeymoon. If you insist on sharing it with Harlowe I can understand why.' He indicated the blackboard behind the bar. 'What do you want to eat?'

'I'm not hungry. Besides, this place is far too expensive for . . . ' She stopped, suddenly embarrassed.

'For what?' he asked, then grinned. 'For a kiss-o-gram man?' he suggested.

She shifted uncomfortably. 'I didn't say that.'

'Not out loud.' He regarded her steadily for a moment and for a moment she thought he was going to say something important. Instead he continued, 'The lamb with rosemary is very good.'

'You come here regularly, of course,' Rosalind snapped.

'I haven't been in Melchester long enough to be a regular anywhere.' The corners of his mouth lifted in a teasing smile. 'Perhaps you could recommend a good spot to do a little busking . . . '

Rosalind exploded and half rose. 'This is ridiculous — '

He caught her hand. 'Gently, Rosie. You don't want to draw attention to yourself, do you?'

For a moment their eyes locked, the brilliant blue against the mystery of her gold and green eyes, until slowly, reluctantly she lowered her lashes before his insistent will. 'You should save your money,' she muttered, obstinately, subsiding into her seat.

Certain that he had finally won her obedience, he allowed the smile to return to his lips, her concern about his financial state apparently amusing him. 'Should I? Whatever for?'

'Rent, perhaps?' she suggested. 'You can't just live from hand to mouth.'

'Is that so?' He seemed genuinely interested. 'I look forward to you telling me why not. I feel sure you're going to.'

'You're irresponsible, Jack Drayton. Did anybody ever tell you that?'

'Ah, Rosie, my irresponsibility is half my charm,' he said with an air of injured innocence. 'But since I don't have to pay rent, you may eat with a clear conscience. Now, what will you have?'

'Don't pay . . . ' She sat back in her chair. 'Do you mean you squat somewhere?' she demanded, horrified.

For a moment the blue eyes flashed with something between humour and exasperation. Humour won. He reached across the table and took her hand in his. 'Would that bother you?' This time she tried harder to pull free, but his long fingers held hers firmly, drawing her nearer to him so that she had no choice but to fight him or follow where he led. When he had her as close as he desired, close enough to see the tiny flecks that darkened the green of her irises, to see how the pupils dilated at his touch, close enough to whisper so that only the two of them could hear, he spoke again. Urgently, now. A little fiercely. 'If I were to tell you that I slept out under the cold winter stars, my darling Rosie, would you take me home and tuck me up under your own downy quilt?'

Rosalind felt the dangerous tug of his charm, the spark of something in his eyes that she seemed to respond to quite mindlessly. She knew just how easy it would be to say yes. How imperative it was she say no. Convincingly. And protesting hadn't worked and her feeble attempts to ignore him had been simply brushed aside. It was time to try a different tack.

She made her answering smile slow, tentative, lowered her lashes suddenly, copying a technique that she and Sarah had used to practise in the mirror for hours when they were teenagers and she had seen her friend use time without number to turn men to putty in her hands. Rosalind had never tried it in earnest until now, and if her lips trembled a little and if maybe it wasn't quite all an act, there was still an almost giddying sense of exhilaration when she heard the sharply indrawn breath that told her she had hit her mark.

'Well now, my darling Jack,' she said, imitating the faintest touch of an Irish lilt that warmed his voice when it was low, 'I'm afraid in those circumstances I'd have to direct you to the nearest branch of the Salvation Army and suggest you throw yourself on their mercy.'

For a moment they were suspended in some place a million miles in space and time from the wine bar. Then Jack broke the spell. 'Is that a fact?' he asked and softly laughed. 'We'll see, sweet Rosie. We'll see.'

Her breath caught in her throat as his eyes held her captive. She tried to speak but no words would come to tell him how wrong he was. Instead the two of them were locked together, their heads inches apart, in a silent battle of wills in which she found herself fighting desperately to control senses racketing wildly out of control.

Then, as if he had seen all he wanted, he released her and sat back. If she could have stood up, she would have walked away. Right then. But her bones had turned to marshmallow and instead she moistened her dry mouth with a sip of the orange juice and made no further protest when Jack ordered for her.

When the waiter had departed, he returned his attention to the holiday brochure on the table in front of him. 'Now, down to business. Where do you want to go for your honeymoon?'

'We haven't decided yet,' she said, finding the subject embarrassing.

'I'm not interested in 'we'. Where do you want to go?'

She swallowed. 'I thought . . . Italy.'

'Italy.' He searched among the brochures. 'A visit to ancient Rome?' he suggested, flipping through the pages. 'The great art galleries of Florence? The treasures of Venice? Funny sort of honeymoon. I don't think Harlowe's mind will be focused on architecture, do you?' He looked up then. 'Or perhaps you're hoping that it will be?' She blushed fiercely and he flicked through the pages of a brochure in front of him with its tantalising views of Rome and Pompeii. 'Is that the plan? To wear the poor old soul out with sightseeing?'

'He's not old!' She wished the floor would simply open and swallow her up. 'Why are you doing this to me?' she asked, hoarsely.

'Anthony Harlowe was born middle-aged. And I'm not doing anything to you. You're doing it to yourself. Why don't you just admit that you've made a mistake before it's too late?'

She lifted her head. 'You're wrong, Jack. I haven't made a mistake. I'm going to marry Anthony because that's exactly what I want.'

'I don't doubt that,' he replied, his eyes flinty. 'In fact I'm sure he's a very good catch. You could put your feet up and never do another day's work for the rest of your life.' He challenged her. 'You might want to marry him, Rosie. That's not precisely the same thing as marrying him because you can't help it. I know you're not in love with him. And he's certainly not in love with you or he would have done something about it by now.'

'Love?' She stared ahead, not seeing anything in the room. Her mother had been in love with her father. She had never complained, never shown by one flicker of her eyelid how much his desertion had hurt. But Rose had suffered pain enough herself to have a very good idea. 'I think you're confusing the emotion with sex.'

'Am I?' His fingers curled under her chin and turned her face towards his. 'Frankly, Rosie, I don't think I'm the one that's confused.' Their food arrived, forcing them apart, and she took refuge in giving her full attention to her lunch and Jack changed the subject. 'Tell me about yourself. Your family.'

She glanced up from the lamb he had ordered for her and found him oddly watchful. 'Not much family,' she said, reluctant to expose herself. 'There's just my mother.'

'What happened to your father?' he asked, idly.

'I no longer have a father.' Her tone indicated an unwillingness to discuss the subject, but he pressed her.

'What do you mean?'

'He got fed up with being grown up and left home,' she said, the flippancy of her remark an attempt to disguise the bitterness she felt. But, seeing Jack's bemused expression, she tried to explain. 'He was a teacher. A music teacher. In his spare time he played a hot jazz piano.' She shrugged. 'He decided that married life, being a husband, a . . . ' she closed her eyes briefly and took a breath ' . . . a father was just not as much fun as playing the clubs, the festivals.' She shrugged, unable to go on. There was a touch of concern in his eyes, but at least he didn't say that he was sorry, for which she was grateful. She had come close to exposing the rawness of her father's desertion. She was glad to change the subject. 'I was wondering . . . if you need work . . . ' He said nothing, waited politely for her suggestion. 'I could speak to Mike Noble. He owns the jazz club; he's an old friend of Dad's. I'm sure he'd listen to you play if I asked.'

'And why would you do that for me, Rosie?'

At last a question that was easy. 'Because you're good, Jack,' she said, with relief. 'Very good. I hate to see all that talent wasted — '

'It's not wasted. I play for my own pleasure, Rosie, and for my friends. I'd

90

play for you any time you asked.'

'Then go to see Mike,' she urged.

He seemed amused by her concern. 'Do I really look as if I need a job?'

No. The truth was that he didn't look as if he needed anything. She dropped her lashes to hide the sharp bittersweet flare of desire. 'You're too good to be wasting your time on . . . ' she blushed, furiously ' . . . your present occupation.'

'Am I?' Jack Drayton looked thoughtful for a moment, then he nodded as if he had come to a decision. 'Very well. But I'll only play if you promise to come and listen.' She began to protest, but he put his hand over hers and stopped her. 'It's my only condition and it's not open to negotiation.' She looked at him then. Braved the clear blue eyes. 'Promise,' he insisted.

Finally, she gave way. 'I promise. It won't be a hardship. I'll ring Mike this afternoon. Have you got a number where you can be reached?'

'Since when have they had telephones in squats?' he teased. 'I'll meet you here for lunch again tomorrow.'

'No.' She had already conceded more than enough and from somewhere she found the strength to be firm. 'I'm not having lunch with you again.'

'Because of Anthony?'

'If the circumstances were reversed you wouldn't be very happy.'

'If the circumstances were reversed, my lovely Rosie, I wouldn't hesitate to rip his head off.'

She gasped and saw him smile. He was teasing her. But she realised just how far she had let herself go in his company. 'Then we must make sure that never happens to you, Jack. You'd find it difficult to play a saxophone without your head,' she said, with forced brightness. 'Ring me at the office in the morning and I'll let you know if I've been able to fix anything.' She wrote the number on the corner of the holiday brochure and handed it to him. 'Thank you for lunch.' She stood up and held out her hand in a gesture that clearly meant goodbye.

He rose to his feet and took the hand she offered and held it. 'I'll walk you back to your office.'

She snatched back her hand. 'No, Jack. Please, stay here until I've gone.' She didn't wait for his answer, but turned and walked quickly away, refusing to look back, even though she found that she wanted to very much indeed.

She phoned the jazz club as soon as she got back. She wanted Jack Drayton out of her mind, she told herself and the sooner she kept her promise the sooner she could forget all about him. Mike was surprised, but pleased to hear from her, and when Rosalind explained why she had rung he laughed, asked if her protégé was her latest boyfriend and, not waiting for her answer, said it would be a pleasure to see Jack any time he called round. Glad that it had been so easy, but relieved, Rosalind buried herself in her work.

It was late when she came out of the office. Outside it was cold and dark and she found the car park slightly alarming when it was so empty with all those dark, echoing spaces.

She hurried up to her car and took the keys from her bag, but before she could insert them in the lock a dark figure detached itself from the shadows and moved towards her. She tried to scream but found she couldn't, her throat constricted, her tongue like wood in her mouth.

'Late tonight, Rosie. Making up for your long lunch?' Jack took the keys from her lifeless fingers and opened the car door for her.

'Damn you, Jack Drayton!' she cried out, when she finally found her voice. 'You frightened the life out of me!'

'Good. You shouldn't be wandering about the car park by yourself at this time of night and you can tell your precious Mr Harlowe that I said so.' He was actually angry, she realised with something of a shock.

'I don't have much choice. I'm a working girl, Jack.'

'It's past eight o'clock, for God's sake! What is the man, a slave-driver?'

'I'm the branch manager. I don't need anyone to drive me, I simply put in the hours I have to. We're short-staffed and I had a lot to catch up on today. And you're right,' she said, somewhat shortly. 'The long lunch hour didn't help.' The fact was that she hadn't realised how late it was, but it was none of his business and she told him so. 'Why are you here, anyway,' she demanded, reaching for her keys.

'Two reasons,' he said, slipping them into his pocket. 'This is the first.' His hands reached for her and caught her shoulders and before she could think what was happening, before she could offer the slightest protest, his mouth had descended on hers.

For a moment she was rigid with shock. But his lips were warm, sweet and arousing as they moved over hers and as his strong arms wrapped around her and held her close against him she found herself responding to him without any thought of the consequences. Her lips parted beneath the gentle probing of his tongue, completely lost to the propriety of her situation as under his sensuous caresses some new longing stirred within her.

She had no idea how long they stood locked together, but when finally he raised his head and looked down at her, his eyes black with desire for the moment held in check, she felt a chill of unease somewhere in her chest. They were alone in an isolated place. She had allowed herself to be lulled by his careless charm, but here, in the almost empty car park, long since abandoned by the city's workers, she was at his mercy. There would be no one to hear her if she called for help . . . A soft cry escaped her lips.

'What's the matter, Rosie? Suddenly remembered Anthony?'

'I . . . no . . . please, just let me go.'

He seemed to recognise the edge of panic in her voice and immediately released her, opening the car door with one smooth movement, his expression a little scornful of her sudden nervousness. She reached for the car door to close it, but he held it, preventing her escape, his face grave.

'You left it rather late to consider the wisdom of trusting a stranger, Rosie. First impressions are sometimes misleading. Not everyone is precisely what he seems to be.'

'Are you speaking personally?' she asked, her voice a little shaky.

'It's the only way I know.' She was unable to see his expression in the shadowy light, but the teasing note was back in his voice, oddly reassuring. She found Jack Drayton in a flirtatious mood a great deal easier to deal with.

'You had a second reason for waiting for me?' she prompted.

'Come to dinner with me first?'

'No, Jack,' she said, with genuine regret. 'I think once is as near the flame as this moth wants to fly.'

The shadows threw his features into

hard angles, giving his face an unexpectedly dangerous edge and the sudden sharpness of his voice rattled against her. 'You must know that, once attracted to the light, my dear Rosie, a moth can never escape.'

The taste of his mouth was still sweet nectar on her tongue. Her wings had already been singed by the heat of this man's passion and he was right. She was in mortal danger of being trapped. 'In this case,' she said, a little breathlessly, 'I'm forced to prove you wrong.'

'Only because I choose to let you go.' He opened the rear door and retrieved his saxophone from the back seat. 'Meanwhile, this is what I came for.'

'Oh,' she said, feeling a little stupid. 'You should have come across to the office this afternoon. I would have given you the keys.'

'My afternoon was devoted to business affairs,' he said, smiling a little at the dangerous flash in her eyes. 'When I went to your flat this evening the girl you share with suggested you might still be working. I did ring the office bell but there was no response.'

'People are always ringing the bell if they see a light. It seems to amuse them. I'm sorry if I've put you to a lot of bother,' she said tightly, then relented. 'Look, I phoned Mike at the club. You can go there any time for an audition.'

'Why don't we go now?' he suggested. 'Then we could — '

'No, thank you,' she said, firmly. 'I said I'd come and listen to you play. Once you've got a job. I think we'd better leave it at that.' He finally allowed her to shut the car door and she felt a great deal safer.

Jack waited for her to move away, a smile curving his generous mouth. She felt in her pocket for her keys and then realised why he was smiling. He swung them on the end of his finger and she wound down the window and held out her hand for them. 'Very funny.'

He made no move to return them to

her. 'I really would like you to come with me now.'

'This isn't funny, Jack. My keys, if you please.'

'Sorry.'

'That's not fair,' she protested.

'I know. But then I've no intention of playing fair,' he replied, evenly. 'So what are you going to do about it, Miss Parry?'

4

Rosalind stared at Jack for a moment and then turned and opened her glove compartment to retrieve her spare set of keys. She started the car and swung it out of the parking bay, then pulled up alongside him. 'That's what I'll do about it, Jack. Perhaps you'll give me back my keys now?'

He laughed. He threw back his head and laughed. It was an infectious sound and despite everything Rose found the corners of her lips lifting in response. Jack tossed the keys in the air, caught them and handed them over with a slight bow. 'Do you know, Rosie,' he said, 'I think I'm going to really enjoy this game.'

'What game?' she demanded.

'Let's call it hot pursuit. I think you'll enjoy it.'

'I very much doubt it,' she snapped

back, furious with herself for asking such a stupid question.

'Just you wait and see.' With that he turned and walked away into the shadows.

As soon as she got home, Sarah pounced. 'All right, Rose. Who is he?'

Rose looked at her flatmate and knew she would get no peace until she at least gave her the bare facts. 'He's a pest, Sarah. An arrogant, oversized, saxophone-playing pest.'

'Tell me more!'

'He's . . . he does those kiss-o-gram things. He came into the office yesterday and played 'Happy Birthday' to me and I haven't been able to shake him off since.'

'Do you want to?' Sarah asked in astonishment.

'Anthony was not very pleased.'

'Who cares what Anthony thinks?' Then she shrugged. 'Well, perhaps you have a point. But if you ever decide to send something like that to me, be kind, send him. Please!'

'I'll bear it in mind,' Rose said, unbending a little.

Sarah brought her a mug of coffee. 'So? Did he?'

'What?'

'Kiss you, silly?'

'Yes, Sarah. He kissed me silly,' she said and actually found herself enjoying the startled look that crossed Sarah's face. 'And before you ask, I'll admit that it was quite an experience.' She sipped the coffee. 'I had lunch with him today.'

Sarah was awestruck. 'No wonder Anthony isn't very pleased.'

'He doesn't know. About the lunch today.'

'Very wise. When are you seeing him again?'

Rose sighed. 'I wish I could say never, but frankly, I'm not very hopeful.' She stood up. 'I'll take this through to the bathroom. I need a soak.'

'I expect I'll be gone by the time you get out. Matt's picking me up after work. I'll stay over there tonight.'

'It's about time you two settled down.'

'Maybe. Perhaps if you marry Anthony I can persuade him to move in here.'

'Not if, Sarah. The first week of May. Tell him to start packing.'

Rose lay back in the bath and tried to forget Jack Drayton, mentally ticking off the things she had to do during the next couple of days. Top of the list was a phone call to her mother to let her know that she and Anthony had finally decided upon a date for the wedding. At least she wouldn't disapprove. After her own unhappy experience her mother understood the qualities that would make Anthony a good husband. He was steady, reliable. She would always know where he was and what he was doing. He would never want to spend his nights playing a piano as long as there was someone willing to listen to him. He would never walk away and leave her without so much as a word.

From the depths of her bath she

heard Matt's arrival and after a considerable amount of hilarity his departure with Sarah who called a brisk cheerio and banged the door behind her.

The water began to cool and she finally forced herself out, and wrapping a towelling robe around her, decided to go and make some toast and take it to bed.

'I prefer your hair like that.' She was halfway to the kitchen when the sound of his voice brought her to an abrupt halt. She stared in disbelief at the back of the battered old wing chair by the fire. But her ears had not deceived her. Jack Drayton was peering around the wing at her. 'Sarah let me in,' he said. 'Nice girl.'

'I'm glad you think so, because she might be in urgent need of somewhere else to live unless you have a very good reason for invading my privacy.'

'Would I bother you without a very good reason, darling Rosie?' His eyes drifted down the contours of her throat and came to a halt where the soft swell of her breasts pushed against her robe. Self-consciously she pulled it tighter.

'Well?' she demanded. 'What is it?'

He rose to his feet and moved towards her. 'You said you'd come and hear me play.' He glanced at his watch. 'And you'll have to hurry and get dressed or I'll be late. I was beginning to think I would have to come and get you out of that bath.'

For a moment the thought of him 'getting her out of that bath' was too distracting to take in what he was saying, then the meaning sank through her befuddled thoughts. 'Mike gave you a chance?'

'Someone rang in sick, apparently. This flu bug that's going round.'

'I'm glad for you, Jack,' she said. She meant it, too, but bit back the flare of excitement that threatened to erupt at the thought of hearing him play again. 'But I can't come with you tonight. It's late. I have to work tomorrow.'

'How did I know you were going to

say that?' He smiled slightly. 'Let me quote you, Rosie. 'I don't make promises that I'm not prepared to keep.' I think I have you exactly?'

Yes. Word for word. 'I know I promised. It's just — '

'It's just that you don't think Anthony would like you to go?'

A wry smile curved her lips. 'I don't think that, Jack. I know it.'

'Then nothing has changed,' he said. 'You must have known that when you made your promise.' She didn't answer. He took a step nearer. 'I'll make you a trade if you like?'

She forced her eyes to meet his. They were too close and she felt vulnerable under their blue power. 'A trade? I don't understand.'

'It's perfectly simple. If you break your promise to marry Anthony, I'll be happy to release you from your promise to me.' The tips of his fingers reached out and touched the smooth curve of her cheek. 'I'll go further, Rosie. I'll stay and tuck you up in bed myself.'

His fingers began to wander down the line of her jaw. Her hand snapped up and caught his wrist. 'What time did you say you had to be at the club?'

'I didn't. But you haven't got long to make up your mind.' He ignored the restraint of her hand on his and effortlessly continued to trail a tiny path of fire with one fingertip towards the cleft of her robe. Briefly, she allowed the sensuous pleasure of the moment to overcome her as burgeoning nipples rose in urgent response to his touch. Her grip on his wrist slackened and she longed for his hand to slide beneath the soft cloth and cup her breast in his long hard fingers. But they halted at the barrier and she opened her eyes, slightly dazed, to find him regarding her with a question in his eyes. She swallowed. 'I'd better go and get dressed,' she said, her voice catching in her throat.

'Yes, Rosie,' he murmured, releasing her. 'I think perhaps you had better.' He took a step back and turned away. 'And if you could make it snappy I'd appreciate it. I'm supposed to be playing in twenty minutes.'

The speed at which she dressed precluded thought and for that she could only be grateful. She hardly even had time to think what she might wear, except that nothing she could lay her hands on seemed right for a jazz club. Desperately she raided Sarah's wardrobe. She wouldn't mind, she thought as she tugged on a pair of black leggings and topped it with a baggy jewel-bright silk shirt. Besides, it was Sarah's fault she was in this predicament.

She brushed out her hair, spent two minutes on her make-up and had to be content with the result. She had run out of time. She stopped in the bedroom doorway and glanced back at the mirror. No. She was more than content. And she smiled. She had promised Jack she would support him and she would. No sulking that he had twisted her arm. The *frisson* of excitement fluttering in her abdomen was proof enough that she hadn't needed more persuasion. And the small tug of guilt that she was actually looking forward to listening to him play was firmly quashed. She was doing nothing to feel guilty about.

Jack's eyes narrowed as she rejoined him in the sitting room. 'Well?' she demanded. 'Are you just going to stand there, Jack Drayton? I thought you were in a hurry.' She threw a thick wrap around her shoulders. 'Shall we go?'

'Yes. I think we'd better.'

His hand was at her back, warm and possessive, as he steered her towards a long, low sports car parked against the kerb.

'This is yours?' she asked in frank disbelief.

'You find it so very difficult to believe I own a Ferrari?' he asked, without rancour.

'I find it difficult to believe that you earn enough doing kiss-o-grams to even pay for the insurance,' she retorted, sharply.

'Then perhaps you should consider the possibility that I don't always stop at kissing,' he suggested, his face expressionless.

She frowned. 'Not . . . ?' Then she coloured fiercely as she realised exactly what he was implying. 'Oh.' His look warned her against pursuing the subject. He opened the door for her and she lay back against the dark leather.

She cleared her throat. She couldn't leave the subject alone. 'Is this the kind of fee you normally . . . ?' She stopped, realising it was a question she couldn't possibly ask.

'Why don't you try me and judge for yourself?' he offered.

'I thought you were in a hurry?' she snapped.

'There are some things it's better not to rush.' But he started the car and turned to her. 'Ready?'

She nodded and held her breath, expecting him to drive off at speed. He didn't. He held the car within the speed limit on the ring road and then they were winding through the city centre. But it was still a breathless experience. Or maybe it wasn't the car at all. Maybe it was just sitting alongside Jack that made her feel weak. They pulled up behind the jazz club and he opened the door for her and took her hand to help her from the car.

'It's a beautiful car,' she said, quickly, feeling that something was required by way of comment. Then, 'Don't you ever want to just put your foot down?'

'When I get overcome with the urge to speed, Rosie, I go to a track. Shall we go in?'

He settled her at a table near the front and went to fetch some drinks and she looked around. It was a long time since she'd been there and the shabbiness of it surprised her. It had the appearance of a place about to fold and that made her sad. She turned her attention to the group on the stage, a quartet backing a girl with a husky voice who had modelled herself on Cleo Laine. Jack slid into the seat beside her and draped his arm along the back of her chair, watching the girl.

'She's good,' Rose whispered.

'She's too young for that song. In a few years, if she sticks with it, she'll be great.' The number came to an end and the girl left the stage. Mike Noble appeared to introduce a guest act. It was a moment before she realised he was talking about Jack.

'Got to go, sweetheart. See you later.' He ran lightly up the steps and on to the stage to some polite applause. He picked up his sax and propped himself on a stool, a figure all in black, picked out by a spotlight. For a moment he stared out at the audience until the room was silent. Then he lifted the instrument to his lips and began to play.

At some point during the performance Mike slipped into the seat beside her. As the last note died away, Rose turned to him and smiled.

'Your friend blows a mean note, Rosie,' he said, as Jack left the stage to a thumping ovation. 'Can you persuade him to come again? It would be nice to go out on a high note.'

'Go out . . . what do you mean? Are you leaving?'

'The bank has invited me to go.' He sat back in his chair. 'I've been losing money for quite a while. I've had an offer from someone who wants to open a snooker club and I think I'd better take it before I lose everything.'

'Hello, Mike. Can I get you a drink?' Jack interrupted.

'No, thanks. I should be buying you one. I was just asking Rose to persuade you to make another date. We might manage a decent crowd for you with a bit of advance publicity.'

'Listen, Mike, I had enough trouble getting her to come out with me tonight . . . ' His eyes said he was joking, but there was a warning edge to his voice.

Mike looked at him and grinned. 'I'll make myself scarce then, but don't think I'll give up. Bye, Rose. Nice to see you.'

'Thanks, Mike.' The words were heartfelt and Mike nodded.

'Any time.'

Rosalind toyed with her glass. 'You were very good.' She had the feeling he wasn't really interested in her views on his playing. 'Mike was impressed. I could tell. What will you do about his offer? Even if the club's closing soon, it could lead to other dates.'

'Could it?' he asked. 'Then I'm tempted.'

'You know what I mean.'

'Yes, I know what you mean. But I'm doing nothing about it until I've danced with you.' He stood up and held out his hand.

Rosalind didn't move. 'You can't go on blackmailing me into doing what you want forever, Jack.'

'Well, let's take it one step at a time and see, shall we? Besides, it would be a shame to waste the rest of the evening.'

'There is no evening left, Jack. I'm usually asleep in bed by this time.'

'If you're offering that as an alternative, I might just change my mind about the dance.' She felt the colour rise to her cheeks, in no doubt that he was serious. Yet she felt under no threat. Despite his relentless pursuit she sensed that he would never take her somewhere she didn't want to go. The problem was that once in his arms she might very well be more than happy to go anywhere he wanted to take her. The thought was rather shocking.

'You're incorrigible,' she scolded.

'More compliments?'

She stood up and he led her to the tiny dance-floor and allowed him to take her into his arms. But the floor was too small to dance properly. He pulled her close and they simply swayed together like most of the other couples, to the rhythm of a sweet clarinet. She tried to keep her mind on the music, but the warm length of his body pressed against her, the feel of hard muscle beneath his thin shirt, the steady beat of his heart against her own, drew her into a warm and hectic circle of enchantment until they were the only two people left in the world.

'Rosie?' She raised her head from his shoulder. 'I think I'd better take you home.'

She lifted her wrist to check the time. It was gone one o'clock, but it wasn't the time that sent a sudden chill through her. It was the watch that Anthony had given her. Yesterday. And now she was wrapped in another man's arms as if there was no tomorrow.

She pulled sharply away from Jack and hurried back to her seat and flung her wrap around her and grabbed her bag, fumbling in her rush so that it slipped from her fingers spilling her belongings across the floor and as she bent to pick it up, Jack bent down too. 'What's the matter?'

'You know what's the matter,' she said, bitterly, carelessly shovelling her belongings back into her bag. 'I shouldn't be here.'

He helped her to her feet, holding

onto her elbows, his laughing eyes suddenly fierce. 'Perhaps you'd better start giving some serious thought about where exactly you do want to be. You can pay too high a price for a little security, Rosie.'

She didn't even bother to dignify this with an answer, but tore herself free from his grasp and turned on her heel, heading quickly for the exit. The club was almost empty, on the point of closing. He unlocked the car door without a word and she climbed in, too angry to speak. He thought she was marrying Anthony for his money, for a soft life. He couldn't be more wrong. She had a good job, didn't need a man to support her. It wasn't financial security she sought.

When they arrived at her home she didn't wait for him to open the door, but got out quickly and began to walk up the stairs to her flat. He followed. She glared at him as he took her elbow and shook him off.

'This is it, Jack,' she said, keeping her

voice down because of the lateness of the hour, but investing her whisper with all the force she could. 'I don't want to see you again.' He said nothing. 'Did you hear me?' she demanded.

'I heard you. You don't want to see me again.'

'Good.' They arrived at the door. Rosalind opened her bag and searched for her keys. They weren't there. For the second time in two days she felt the urge to stamp her foot.

'What's the matter?'

'I've lost my keys.'

'Perhaps you dropped them in the car,' he suggested. 'I'll go and see.'

'I'll come with you. Then there will be no need for you to come back upstairs.'

He shrugged. 'If you like.' But the keys weren't in the car. 'They must have fallen out when you dropped your bag. You'll just have to knock up Sarah.'

'I can't. She's . . . ' She was unwilling to say where Sarah was. He was quite capable of taking it as an invitation.

'She's staying at a friend's.'

'I can see that she wouldn't appreciate being disturbed, then.' He laughed softly and too late Rose remembered that he had seen Sarah and Matt leave together. 'Well, you can't stand out here in the rain all night. Hop back in the car and I'll take you to the club.'

She had no choice, but she climbed very unwillingly back into the Ferrari. And it didn't do any good. The club was in total darkness when they arrived and Jack's hammering only brought a security patrol to ask them what they were about.

Rosalind felt like crying. It was all so ridiculous. She couldn't even fling the blame at Jack, much as she would have liked to. She had been so desperate to get away from him that she had almost run out of the place without bothering to check that she had everything.

'Is there somewhere I can take you? Your mother's?'

'She lives nearly thirty miles away.'

'I'll take you, nevertheless, if that's

what you want.'

She shook her head. 'It's too far. I have an appointment at nine in the morning.' She looked in despair at her clothes. 'I wonder what time the cleaners come in?'

'Loath as I am to suggest this, what about Anthony?' Her startled glance was sufficient. Turning up on Anthony's doorstep in the middle of the night escorted by Jack Drayton wouldn't do much for their relationship. Always supposing she could think of some convincing reason why they should be together. 'No? You don't think he'd understand. Perhaps not. Well, there's nothing left, Rosie. You'll just have to come home with me.'

'I can't do that!'

'Can't you?' he mocked her. 'Have you a sensible alternative? There's a fine cardboard box over there. I'm sure the rats will be willing to share.'

She shuddered. 'There must be something else I can do.'

'It's two o'clock in the morning,

sweetheart. I'll leave you to think about it. In the meantime . . . ' He started the car and pulled out into the road. The streets were almost empty. Black and shiny with rain, but Rosalind didn't notice. She only knew that she was getting deeper and deeper into Jack Drayton's nets and the more she struggled, the tighter they bound her.

Half an hour later they pulled into a small courtyard. The house looked familiar. But she saw so many houses and she could hardly keep her eyes open.

'Up to bed with you.' He pushed her up the stairs and into a large room with a double bed. It was clearly his room and she nervously backed away. 'The bathroom's through there, Rosie. I'll see you in the morning.' He shut the door firmly and she heard his feet clattering down the stairs.

That was it? Not even an attempt to join her in the huge double bed? She wasn't sure whether to feel relieved or insulted. Or was that part of his game?

She looked at the bed doubtfully. It was inviting and she was tired, but once under its soft covers she would be at Jack Drayton's mercy. Just because he walked away now, it didn't mean he might not come back. Rose glanced at the door and confirmed that there was no lock, but there was a small chair and she propped it under the handle. Feeling decidedly safer she went through to the bathroom. It was beautiful. Richly panelled in pink and white marble. She did know the house but she was just too tired to think about it. Right now all she cared about was falling into bed. She stripped off her clothes and climbed beneath the duvet and was asleep in a minute.

* * *

It was the rattling of the door handle that woke her. For a minute she had no idea where she was. The light was coming in at the wrong angle. And that was wrong too. She was up before daylight at this time of year. She lay surrounded by strange things, in a strange bed, and tried to gather her wits.

'Rosie?'

At the sound of his voice it all came flooding back to her. She was lying in Jack Drayton's bed without a stitch of clothing on and he was trying to get in.

'Go away!'

'It's half-past eight. I've brought you some breakfast.'

She shot up, wrapped the quilt around her and pulled the chair away from the door. She half opened it. Jack was wearing a dark silk dressing-gown and holding a tray. 'Half-past eight?'

'You looked exhausted last night. I let you sleep on.'

'You had no right to do that. Oh, lord, what a mess!' She made a grab for her clothes and he came in and set the tray down beside the bed.

'I phoned the club. Mike has your keys. I said I'd pick them up later.' He waited. ' 'Thank you, Jack?' ' he prompted.

She didn't take the hint. She wasn't ready to be friends with Jack Drayton. It caused too much trouble.

'It was the least you could do under the circumstances.'

'I didn't lose your keys, Rosie,' he reminded her. 'Tell me, are you always this bad-tempered in the morning? Or have I done something to upset you?'

'I'm not bad-tempered.' Her voice rose dangerously. 'But if you will leave now, I'd like to get dressed.'

He shrugged. 'Then it must be me, although I can't think why. Come and have a cup of tea.'

'I have an appointment ten miles out of the city at nine o'clock this morning, Jack.'

'Then unless you plan to attend it dressed in the eye-catching outfit you were wearing last night,' he replied, 'you're not going to make it.' He indicated the phone. 'I suggest you call your office and delegate.'

She glowered at him. 'I don't really have much choice, do I?'

'Not really.'

She stared at the phone, then shrugged and trailed back to the bed, hugging the quilt around her. But it was the simple solution and she spoke to Julie who worked flexible hours to fit around arrangements for her children and often started early. She arranged for one of the negotiators to meet her prospective purchasers at the house in Wickham.

'That wasn't so difficult, was it? Now you can have your breakfast without a worry in the world.' He handed her a cup of tea and she sipped it. 'Toast? I couldn't find any marmalade.'

'I hate marmalade.'

'Well, that's a relief.' He offered a smile and she found herself returning it. Apparently taking this as a truce, he sat on the side of the bed and helped himself to a slice. She shrugged and followed suit. There was no point in starving. And there was no point in blaming Jack for a situation which, as he had taken pains to point out, was entirely her own fault. Besides, she was still very much at his mercy. She would need a lift home.

She glanced at her watch. 'Will you take me to the club now, Jack? I really must go home and get some clothes.'

'If you insist. Although frankly I like you the way you are.'

'Wrapped up in a quilt?'

'Just like Christmas. Are you one of those careful unwrappers, Rosie? Or do you like to tear the paper off your parcels in a frenzy of excitement?'

Certain that this conversation had nothing to do with Christmas parcels, she lifted her chin a little. 'Christmas is over.'

'There's always next year. It's as well to be prepared.' He stood up. 'Meantime you want to go home. Can you spare me the bathroom while you finish off the toast?' He ran a hand over a bristle-dark chin. 'I didn't think to move my things from there last night.'

'Help yourself.'

He looked at her for a moment, then

shook his head. 'I'm sure you don't mean half the things you say.'

She hurled a pillow at him. He caught it and held it for a moment against his face. 'It has your scent.'

Rose frowned. 'I wasn't wearing any scent.'

'Not the kind you dab behind your ears, Rosie. You. Your skin. Your hair.' He tossed the pillow back at her. 'If you could bottle that you would be a millionaire.'

He didn't wait for her answer. He closed the bathroom door and after a moment she heard the shower running. She lay back against the pillow. She turned her face to it and tried to catch a scent, then silently berated herself for a fool.

She looked at her watch. It was nearly nine and she was anxious to get home and changed and into the office. She had already had to ask someone to take one of her appointments, something she considered very unprofessional. The house in Wickham was a major property and all viewings had to be accompanied because the owner was abroad. The way a house was shown could make all the difference to a possible sale.

It was very quiet and she wondered idly where they were. She had only caught a glimpse of the house in the headlights of the car last night and now listened intently, hoping for some sound that might give her a clue. The shower had stopped, but Jack apparently sang while he shaved and he must have left a radio on somewhere because she could hear voices.

She frowned. The voices appeared to be coming nearer. She sat up in bed, suddenly nervous. 'Jack?' she called, as loudly as she dared.

He opened the bathroom door and for a moment she forgot everything else. He was naked but for a white towel wrapped around his hips, his hair still wet from the shower, a smear of shaving foam clinging to his throat. A fine dark scattering of hair arrowed upward from his navel to spread across a broad tanned chest. Dressed, he was impressive. Like this, he was magnificent.

'What is it, Rosie?'

His question and the sound of a door shutting nearby brought her back to earth with a thump. 'There's someone out there,' she hissed.

There was a murmur of voices from beyond the door and as they both turned to stare at it, it began to open.

5

'Jack!' she whispered urgently, heart in her mouth. He moved protectively towards her, taking her hand. It was an infinitely comforting gesture.

'This is the master bedroom, beautifully fitted with an en-suite bathroom . . . ' Anthony swept the door open and gestured generally.

'Get under the quilt,' Jack hissed at Rose, but too late. Anthony turned away from whoever he was talking to and as his startled eyes swept the room they met those of Rosalind, her exposed shoulders proclaiming her nudity, clutching the duvet protectively to her breast and the glowing description of the room abruptly halted. As if unable to believe the scene before him, his gaze shifted to Jack. Bare-legged, bare-chested, only the towel wrapped around his hips between him and total exposure. Despite this disadvantage, he was the first to find his voice.

'Good morning, Harlowe. Trifle early for social calls isn't it?'

Anthony, his eyes riveted upon the scene before him, opened his mouth. Apparently unable to think of anything to say that would cover the situation, he closed it again. He blinked at Rosalind as if trying to clear a mist, as if he wasn't quite sure that he could believe his own eyes. There was a movement behind him. 'If we could just see the room, Mr Harlowe?'

'By all means,' Jack invited, cordially. 'Do come in. The more the merrier.'

A middle-aged couple pushed past Anthony and stared at the two by the bed. 'The bathroom is through there,' Jack said, inviting them with a gesture to help themselves, his eyes never leaving Anthony. 'Beautifully panelled in Breschia marble,' he offered, in the favoured jargon of estate agents. 'Bath with jacuzzi, shower stall — large enough for two — twin basins, fitted mirrors and bidet. There may be some water on the floor so be careful not to slip. The shower leaks,' he added, confidentially.

'Does it?' The man glanced at his wife and they immediately seized upon this excuse. 'Well, the house isn't quite . . . er . . . and leaky showers . . . difficult . . . I think we've seen enough, Mr Harlowe.' The pair backed out rapidly, leaving Anthony to cope with the situation as best he could.

But this diversion had given Anthony time to locate his voice. 'I want an explanation of this. Rosalind!'

Jack intervened. 'Leave it, Harlowe. This is not the moment. You'd better go after your customers.'

'I have nothing to say to you.' His eyes were fixed on Rosalind.

'I can explain . . .'

Jack squeezed her hand reassuringly. 'You don't have to, Rosie. In the circumstances I think it might be better not to try. He won't believe you. At least not until he's had a chance to calm down.'

'Damn you, Jack!' she said, snatching her hand away. 'You're loving every minute of this, aren't you?'

Jack did not bother to deny it. Instead he moved across the room towards Anthony. 'I think it's time you left,' he said quietly. 'If Miss Parry wants to dignify whatever you're thinking with an explanation, she can do it later. Right now, you're the third one who's a crowd in my bedroom.'

'This, sir, is not your bedroom,' Anthony exploded. 'You are trespassing and I will have the full force of the law on you. Rosalind, get dressed and I'll take you home,' he ordered.

Rosalind shuddered as she thought of the clothes she had worn to the jazz club the night before. They would probably shock Anthony almost as much as this situation. And, however much she hated to agree with Jack at this moment, she sensed that he was probably right. Anthony needed time to cool down. Once he had time to think, he would realise that there must be a reasonable explanation. That there had to be an explanation for behaviour so totally out of character. But she needed to gather her wits, put on a little armour before she faced him with it. 'I'll see you later, Anthony.'

His lips tightened. 'Very well. But I warn you that our future together is now in serious doubt. And so, after this débâcle, is your job.'

They waited silently, listening to Anthony's murmur of apologies to the couple who had come to view the house. The front door banged, then two cars started up and left. Rosalind let out a long shuddering sigh.

Jack looked across at her, a touch of something like pity in his eyes. 'Would he really sack you?'

'For using a house entrusted to our care as a . . . as a . . . ' She refused to put into words what Anthony obviously thought they had used it as. 'I think he'd be entitled to, don't you?'

'It wasn't your fault, Rosie. You had no idea.'

'Not much of an excuse, Jack.' Besides, the arrival of Anthony had stirred her memory. She knew exactly where she was now. There was a certain irony to the situation. She was just where she was supposed to be. Showing that couple over this house. 'In this case, it's no excuse at all. The owner is away and Anthony is right. You are trespassing and, what is worse, you've made me your unwitting accomplice.' She glared at him, suddenly furious with him, furious with herself for being so stupid. 'Is the car stolen too, Jack?' she said, bitterly. 'Will we be stopped by the police on the way into Melchester?'

His face gave nothing away, but there was a diamond-hard edge to his voice. 'Since there's no other way of getting into the city, sweetheart, you'll have to take that chance, won't you?'

'I'll call a cab,' she said, recklessly.

'You could,' he agreed. 'But I fancy friend Harlowe will waste no time in calling the police. I'm sure he's got a phone in his car. Since I have no wish to involve you in that sort of scene I suggest we belay the recriminations and move. Right now.' He gathered some clothes from the closet. 'Help yourself to the bathroom.' He paused in the doorway on the way out and grinned. 'By the way, I was lying about the shower.' She reached out and hurled the first thing that came to hand. He fielded the alarm clock with ease and placed it out of harm's way on the tallboy. It went off as he quietly closed the bedroom door.

For a moment she stared at it, then flew out of bed, turned it off and had the quickest shower in history. She pulled on the leggings, wincing at the gaudy shirt, at the girl who had worn it last night with such a careless disregard for the consequences.

'Rosie? Are you ready?' he called.

She gave up any attempt to do something with her hair. 'I'm coming.'

Downstairs, dressed in last night's clothes, hair tousled, watching Jack back the Ferrari out of the garage, she felt cheap. As if she had done the things that Anthony imagined. She looked up at the golden façade of the house, the mellow stones reflecting the winter sunlight. What on earth had made Jack pick this place to squat in? A certain sense of style, perhaps. Natural good taste.

Jack opened the car door. 'Come on, Rosie. Time to face the music.'

She turned away reluctantly. 'I love this house,' she said, with a sigh.

'Better ask Harlowe to buy it for you, then.'

'No. When we're married . . . ' She paused, closed her eyes to blot out the expression in Anthony's eyes when he had seen her in that enormous bed. 'If we get married, we'll live with his mother. She doesn't want to move and the house is very big . . . '

Jack's expression said it all. 'Does he have any idea what you're really like under that prim exterior you've gone to such pains to cultivate for him, Rosie?' He shook his head. 'Marry him if you must. But I give it a month. And I'm being optimistic.'

It was probably academic, she thought, miserably. Anthony had a very strict idea of how his future wife should behave. A night trespassing with an irresponsible musician would be very high on his list of undesirable activities. Assuming she could convince him that was all she had done. She looked back at the house. 'I hope whoever buys it will be happy here.'

'So do I, Rosie,' he said, with feeling. 'So do I.'

She was unhappy about getting into the Ferrari. Last night it had seemed dark, sleek, beautiful, almost discreet. In broad daylight it was a vivid scarlet streak of danger. Everyone in the world would turn to look at it. But there was no alternative, she had to risk it. Something she seemed to be doing ever since Jack had erupted into her office, into her life. Well aware of her reluctance, Jack said, 'I promise I'll keep to the speed limit. Then they won't have an excuse to stop me.'

'Is that why you were so careful last night?' she retaliated. She had actually thought highly of him for resisting the urge to speed on the ring road. Not too many drivers bothered about the limit.

'No,' he said. 'I just enjoy being in your company and the slower I drive, the longer I have you all to myself.'

'Will you stop it! Haven't you done enough damage already?'

He glanced at her. 'That has to be seen. I certainly hope so.'

Ten minutes later they passed a police car speeding in the direction of Wickham. Rosalind gave an unconscious wail of anguish.

'Don't fret, Rosie. Harlowe won't have shopped you. I'm a big enough target to satisfy him.'

'In his shoes I think I might have.'

'No, Rosie, in his shoes you'd have punched me on the nose.'

She glared at him, furious with him for being so right. It was her nature to react without thinking. A dangerous nature and he was right when he suggested that she had taken every effort to tame it. But given the situation that faced Anthony this morning she knew she would have exploded. Jack glanced at her. 'I'm right, aren't I?'

'You needn't be so smug about it.'

'I'm not. But you've more spirit in your little finger, Rosie, than Harlowe has in his entire overstuffed frame.'

'Lucky for you,' she growled.

'You're assuming that I'd have let him hit me.'

'The situation would never have arisen. He's not like that, Jack. He's a gentleman.'

'Is he?' He shrugged. 'I didn't see too much evidence of it this morning. But I'm sure you're right in suggesting that he's too careful to get involved in a brawl. Just as he's too careful to do anything to get Nightingale and Drake bad publicity. I expect he's already regretting his call to the local constabulary. I can see the headlines in the Melchester *Chronicle*. 'Estate Agent Uses House for Secret Love Tryst'.

That wouldn't do much for confidence, would it?'

She buried her face in her hands. 'He'll think I let you have the keys.'

'Wouldn't surprise me,' he agreed, apparently unconcerned at the fate that awaited her. 'He isn't very bright, is he?'

She ignored this, but frowned. 'How *did* you get the keys?'

'I wondered how long you would take to get around to that question.' He turned to her briefly at the traffic lights. 'Would you believe that I simply knocked next door and told them I was a friend of the owner? That he said I could stay for a few weeks while I was in the area?'

She stared at him. The honest blue eyes, the firm mouth and chin. Yes. She could believe it. She hadn't thought of herself as gullible, and look what a mess she was in. 'What did they say?'

'Any friend of John's is a friend of ours. If you need anything just shout and why don't you drop by for a drink this evening?' he said.

'You mean they didn't ask you to stay for dinner?' There was a bitter edge to her voice.

'Well, yes, as a matter of fact they did. After a few drinks. They're really very nice people.'

'And you took advantage of them. You are the most dreadful man I've ever had the misfortune to meet.'

The corners of his mouth creased in amusement. 'I play a mean horn, though.'

'Yes,' she agreed, with a sigh. 'You certainly play a mean horn. That should have been enough to warn . . . ' She stopped before she betrayed herself too completely. Jack called in at the club to fetch her keys. Then he drove her home.

He opened the car door for her and made a move to accompany her upstairs. 'No, Jack. Don't come up.'

'If you're sure?'

'Perfectly.' She held out her hand. 'And I'll take the keys, Jack.'

'Keys?'

143

'You know what I mean. The house keys. Or did you think I'd let you go back?'

He grinned. 'You're learning fast, sweetheart. But what about my clothes?'

She tried to ignore the fact that he was standing very close, that even out here on the cold pavement she responded to the nearness of his body in a way that disturbed and bothered her. 'You won't want to run into the police, Jack. I'll go back tonight and clear up and I'll pack your things,' she said, crisply.

He took her chin in his hand and tilted it up until she was forced to face his scrutiny. 'You'd do that for me, Rosie?'

The touch of his fingers against her skin sent a tremor through her body. While he had had her at his mercy he had made no move to touch her, except to hold her hand in a simple gesture of comfort. Now, when she was home free, he chose to remind her of that spark that had flashed between them. Yes, she thought. Oh, yes. She would do that for him. But he must never know.

'No, Jack,' she said. 'I'm doing it for me. The fewer people who know about this, the better. Do you have any suitcases?' she added, with a briskness she was far from feeling.

For a moment his eyes held her. 'Two black jobs. You'll find them in the wardrobe. They are labelled.'

She nodded. 'You can pick them up here at eight o'clock tonight. And I'll warn the neighbours against letting you back in, so you needn't try any stories about losing your keys.'

'You're a hard woman. I really liked that house.' He smiled slightly. 'I may yet have to throw myself on your mercy. After all, I took you in when you had nowhere to stay.'

'You said it, Jack,' Rose snapped back. 'I'm a hard woman and I really like my job, too. But I may not have one after this morning's little escapade.'

Jack gave her a long look. 'If I didn't know better, darling Rosie, I might

145

think that you're a great deal more concerned about your job, than whether you're still about to become Mrs Anthony Harlowe.'

'That's not true,' she retorted, fiercely, refusing even to consider the possibility that he might be right.

'No? Well, I shouldn't worry too much. You'll have to do a bit of fast talking, but I don't think Anthony will be telling too many people that he found his betrothed in bed with another man, do you?'

She gasped. 'I wasn't in bed with you!'

'A fine distinction. You were, after all, in my bed.' He held out a bunch of keys on the tip of his finger. 'I hope you can persuade Anthony that there is a difference. If you need any help, be sure to let me know.'

'Don't you think you've already done enough?' She snatched the keys. 'Goodbye, Jack,' she said, turning away with determination and heading for the entrance to the flats.

'Until this evening,' he reminded her. She didn't look back but ran up the stairs to her apartment. It would be a very brief meeting this evening, she promised herself. She had done her last good deed as far as Jack Drayton was concerned. His type was nothing but trouble. She had known it from the beginning but had ignored all the danger signals.

Now she had to try to salvage something from the wreckage. Despite Jack's confidence, she had very little doubt that Anthony would want to forget the wedding plans, at least for the moment and she could hardly blame him. She had behaved very stupidly. But she didn't have time to worry about that. Right now she had to set about convincing Anthony that she would never do anything like it again. Because Jack was certainly right about one thing. Her job mattered to her a great deal.

★   ★   ★

Anthony listened grim-faced to her halting story. She left nothing out and made no excuses. She told him about her lunch with Jack. How she had arranged an audition at the jazz club. About leaving her keys behind. Finally she placed the keys to the Wickham property on his desk. 'I will clean up any mess in the house this evening after the office closes.'

'I knew the man was trouble. I warned you, Rosalind.'

'You were right, Anthony,' she said, her throat tight with misery at having to admit how wrong she had been. 'I should have listened to you.'

'You can't help some people.'

'No.'

'I do admire you for trying.' This was so unexpected that she frowned. 'And I choose to believe that you didn't . . . do anything to prevent our wedding going ahead as planned.' Choose? The word suggested room for doubt, she thought. 'But I want your promise that you will never see the man again.'

She hesitated. She considered explaining that she had to see Jack once more to hand over his bags. But it would only take a moment. It wasn't the sort of meeting that Anthony meant. Yet to make such a promise seemed almost a tacit admission of some kind of guilt.

'I don't think I can make a promise like that, Anthony. You either trust me or you don't.'

He stared at her as if he was seeing her for the first time. The silence lengthened between them. 'What have you done about the police?' she said, finally.

He looked relieved that she had asked something he could deal with. 'I've withdrawn my complaint. Told them it was a misunderstanding. There's no need to take it any further under the circumstances.' Rose found herself breathing a soft sigh of relief. Then chided herself. She was doing it again. Worrying about Jack Drayton. Trying to protect him. 'But I think it might be a good idea to check on any other properties that are empty,' Anthony went on, 'in case he tries the same thing again. I'll have to do it myself, it's not the sort of thing we want every junior negotiator finding out about. But it'll have to be this evening as we're so short-handed. If this epidemic keeps up we'll be the only two still working,' he added, with an attempt at humour.

'Yes, Anthony.' Her head was beginning to ache quite dreadfully. 'If there's nothing else I'd better get to my desk.'

'Yes, of course. The staff are very pushed. I don't know how we would have managed without Julie today. She's a very capable woman.' His tone suggested that she could learn something from her example.

Grateful that he had at last recognised Julie's qualities, Rose ignored the implied criticism, happy to agree. 'Yes, she is.'

'I'm just off to the East Street branch. They're apparently down to one man and he sounded dreadful on the phone.'

'Anthony — ' She wanted to explain.

He was a proud man and it must have been hard to forgive her the embarrassment she had caused.

'Yes?' He looked up from a paper that had already claimed his attention, a touch of impatience in his voice.

'Nothing.'

She staggered down the stairs and almost fell into her chair. Julie handed her a cup of coffee. 'Do you want to talk about it?'

'What?'

'Mr Harlowe came back from Wickham with a face like thunder. And after being closeted with him for half an hour, you look like death. Have vandals got in and messed the place up?'

'Vandals?' she said. 'Oh, no. Nothing like that. A . . . a squatter, that's all. It's been dealt with. There's no damage.' At least not to property. Her self-esteem had taken something of a battering. 'Don't mention it to anyone else. It wouldn't do our image much good if it got out. Have you got such a thing as an aspirin?'

Julie found a box in her desk and gave her a glass of water. 'Are you finally succumbing to the bug that's going round?'

Rose made an effort at a smile. Her face was aching with the effort, but it seemed to convince Julie. 'Not me. Constitution of a horse.' She shook herself. 'Where is everybody?'

'Mark and Susie have called in with the flu. That's why I had to telephone Mr Harlowe at home and ask him to do the viewing in Wickham,' she added apologetically. 'Everyone else is out.'

'And I chose today to be late. Sorry, Julie.'

'We coped. But tomorrow is the property section in the paper.'

'I'll see if I can get a temp to help with the phones.'

'I've tried the agencies already. Nothing doing. Everyone's in the same boat. Shall I ask my sister if she'll do Saturday?'

'Please. She could come in after school tomorrow if she would like to.

She could help . . . ' She put her hand to her throat which seemed to be constricted. Julie looked at her oddly.

'Are you sure you're all right?'

'Fine.' It was just the dull ache of tears unshed. But there was no time to indulge in self-pity, and guilt kept her pinned to her desk without a break for the remainder of the day. At least the constant battle to keep ahead of the phones pushed Jack Drayton to the back of her mind. But by the end of the day, as she set off for Wickham, her eyes were gritty and her head was splitting.

She let herself into the house and set about the task of erasing all signs of Jack's presence. She stripped the bed she had slept in and a single bed in the room next door and put the linen in the washing machine. While the wash cycle was running she looked for the two large black suitcases and found them in the wardrobe, labelled, as he had promised: Jack Drayton, Inn on the Park, London. For a moment she was confused. Then she began to fling his clothes into them. Just another of his little tricks, she thought crossly. Probably to convince the next door neighbours of his probity. Not that there was anything cheap about the luggage, she decided. Or his clothes.

They were mostly casual things it was true, but his sweaters had the unmistakable feel of cashmere and there was a beautifully tailored dinner jacket. Then she pulled a face. Probably *de rigueur* for a con man. She folded it carefully on the top, then checked the rest of the house for anything she had overlooked. She spotted the silk dressing-gown across the chair in the spare bedroom and picked it up. She shook it out and folded it and as she bent over the suitcase with it caught an indefinable scent that reminded her so painfully of him that she slammed the lid shut and fastened it before she was tempted to bury her face in it and cry her eyes out.

Her limbs felt leaden as she cleared away the remains of their meagre breakfast. She washed up and put everything away and emptied the refrigerator. She wiped it out and leaned against it briefly to cool her hot cheek. Her head was throbbing and her throat seemed to have closed. She looked in her bag for the aspirins Julie had given her and took two more before calling next door to explain Jack's abrupt departure. She decided to tell them that he had been called away on business, with perhaps just a gentle hint that they contact the office should anyone else turn up.

She rang the bell, shivering on the doorstep. But in the event her story was unnecessary. The neighbours were out and on reflection she thought it was just as well. The police might have spoken to them already and given them an entirely different version of events. She left a note for the milkman with five pounds and hoped that would cover the bill, loaded her car and thankfully headed home.

The flat was empty. Sarah had been back and left a note tucked in the hall mirror. 'Matt's got the bug. I'll be over at his place looking after him if you need me. Love, Sarah.' Rose shivered and turned on the fire and went to make some tea. She was pouring the boiling water on the tea when the doorbell rang and she jumped and it splashed on her hand.

She stifled a moan and went to answer the door. Jack started forward as he saw her nursing her hand, saw her face.

'Whatever is the matter?'

'Nothing. I just . . . ' She glanced at her hand. 'It's nothing.'

He caught her hand and looked at it and, disdaining to comment on her diagnosis, hurried her into the kitchen and stuck it under cold running water. The water was freezing. Far worse than the burn, but he wouldn't let her remove her hand and she felt too weak to resist.

'Your bags . . . ' she began. Her mouth kept moving but the words refused to come out.

Jack removed her hand from the water and looked at it. 'How does that feel?'

She tried clearing her throat. 'I . . . ' It happened again and he looked up and frowned.

'Are you all right, Rosie?' he asked. 'You're rather pink.'

'I'm fine,' she croaked. 'Just take . . . ' This was ridiculous. She had refused to promise Anthony that she would never see him again. But she had promised herself. Her voice ignored the signals from her brain. She gestured hopelessly with her free hand and he clamped his over her forehead.

'My dear girl, you're on fire,' he said. 'There's only one place for you and that's your bed.'

'No . . . ' She mouthed the word, but no sound came. But she had to convince him. She was never ill. Constitution of a horse. She tried to tell him, but her voice had given up the struggle.

'I'm not having any argument, Miss

157

Rosalind Parry,' he warned. 'To bed with you.' She shook her head furiously and then wished she hadn't as the room spun and the pain behind her eyes intensified. She grabbed for his shoulders to prevent herself from falling, but her legs were like butter and as she slithered down him, he scooped her up and carried her swiftly through to her room and laid her upon the bed. She knew she should get up. This was all wrong. But her limbs would not obey her.

Jack eased off her shoes and jacket. Then turned his attention to the zip of her skirt and she began to protest. But it hurt to move her head. It hurt to move everything.

'Keep still, Rosie,' he muttered. 'I'm putting you to bed, not taking you to bed. There's a world of difference.' He briskly dealt with her skirt and slip, then glanced around for a nightgown. She lay in skimpy silk underwear, quite beyond caring. He propped her up, slipped a girlish white gown over her head and then removed her bra before poking her arms through the appropriate holes. That done, he laid her back down and after that the world went black.

6

Rosalind opened her eyes a crack, winced at the light seeping in around the door from the hall and closed them again. She ached everywhere and her skin was burning. There was a movement by her bed.

'Sarah?' she murmured, and moaned softly at the pain in her throat.

'Ssh. Don't try to talk.' A cool cloth bathed her face and neck. 'Drink some of this, Rosie.' A strong arm propped her up and she drank thirstily from the glass held to her lips before she caught the bitter taste of aspirin and tried to push it away. 'Finish it up,' the voice insisted and she did as she was told, shuddering as it went down. 'Good girl.' She lay back against the pillow, weak with the effort and the duvet was drawn up over her and tucked around her shoulders. 'Try to get some more sleep.'

She didn't need encouraging to close her eyes. She drifted off. Woke shivering and clutched at a hot water bottle that was tucked in beside her. She dreamed once that Jack was bending over her anxiously, applying a cold cloth to her face and neck, and in her dream she tried to thank him but the words wouldn't come. He smiled as if he understood and oddly that helped.

Time passed, disturbed, painful. Bouts of shivering alternated with periods of overheating so intense that she threw off her covers. Cool soothing drinks helped her throat. She clung to hot water bottles that magically never seemed to cool.

She finally woke soaked with sweat, her hair clinging in lank strands about her face. The night had been long and dreadful, but now it was day and she had to get to work. Rosalind marshalled her strength and tried to get out of bed. For a moment she sat on the edge of the bed, waiting until the room stopped spinning. Then she stood up.

'Rosie! I take my eyes off you for two minutes and you're in trouble.' Jack helped her up off the floor and on to the bed, wrapping her up in the quilt as she began to shiver uncontrollably.

'Jack?' She'd been dreaming about him and now he was in her bedroom. She didn't understand. 'What are you doing here?' she managed to croak.

'Looking after you.'

'I don't need looking after.' She tried to sit up and he helped her, propping her up against his chest. 'I don't need looking after,' she insisted, so weakly that even she didn't believe it.

'Don't waste your breath, Rosie. Drink this.' She sipped the orange juice he held for her.

'Where's Sarah? You can't . . . ' This last effort was too much for her throat and it refused to co-operate further.

'I found a note stuck in the mirror. She's apparently looking after Matt and if he's only half as bad as you, he needs her. Come on. I'll help you to the bathroom. That is where you were trying to get to, I imagine?' He didn't wait for confirmation. 'Then it's back to bed with you and no argument.'

'I have to get to work,' she managed.

'Shall we see if you can make it to the bathroom first?' he suggested.

She made it to her feet and for a moment thought everything would be fine, but as soon as he removed the steadying arm her legs began to buckle and in the end she had to give in to the humiliation of being helped. But once in the bathroom she hung on to the towel rail and stubbornly refused any further assistance. 'I can manage,' she said.

Jack gave her a searching look. 'Don't lock the door,' he warned.

If her face hadn't been hurting so much she would have laughed. It took every ounce of strength to get to the toilet. She didn't have any left over to waste on locking doors.

Afterwards she tried to wash. But she

couldn't even turn on the tap. She was shivering, damp with sweat from the effort of getting so far and she clung shakily to the basin for support, staring angrily at her reflection in the mirror. A gaunt white face she hardly recognised stared back, eyes huge in dark circles. She hated to be so helpless. She was never ill. How dared her body let her down like this? It was only willpower that was keeping her on her feet. Before she could stop them, huge hot tears rolled down her cheeks and splashed against the porcelain.

Jack's voice, urgent outside the door, elicited no response. He called again, then opened the door. He took one look at her and without ceremony swept her up into his arms and carried her back to bed.

He had found fresh sheets and pillow cases in the airing cupboard and remade the bed. Then he shook out a clean nightdress and without any fuss stripped her of the damp rag she was wearing and replaced it. He covered her with the quilt and she lay back, exhausted.

But he hadn't quite finished. He made her drink some more painkillers.

'Go away, Jack.' The words were feeble, but he understood them.

'You'll have to throw me out, Rosie. And I think twice in one week is a bit much even for you.' But she was so distressed that he sat on the edge of the bed and gently wiped away the tears that trickled down her cheeks with the smooth pad of his thumb. 'Is there anyone else who can look after you?' He hesitated. 'I could ask Sarah to call Anthony.'

She shook her head, tried to speak but was racked with a fit of coughing. She finally caught her breath. 'He's needed at the office. Short-staffed.'

'Surely you're more important than his business?' he asked, with just a touch of impatience. She couldn't be bothered to explain. She was too exhausted. 'What about his mother?'

She shook her head, once. Anthony's

mother had a morbid fear of illness. She hadn't been outside the house since the flu epidemic had begun. If she could only think. There must be some solution. But her head hurt and she felt so weak. She just wanted to close her eyes and forget everything. When she woke again the curtains were drawn against the night.

Jack had fallen asleep in the wing chair he had brought in from the living room. There were deep shadows beneath his eyes and he desperately needed a shave. A dark lock of hair had fallen over his forehead and he looked, she thought, oddly vulnerable. A newspaper he had been reading by the light of a small lamp, lay open on his lap and as she watched began to slide inexorably towards the floor.

She made a move to catch it before it fell and woke him, but he opened his eyes and retrieved it and folded it. 'Hello, sleepyhead,' he said. 'How do you feel?'

'Better, I think.' Her voice was still

croaky, but she no longer felt as if she was trying to talk at long distance through a tube. He leaned over her and placed a cool hand on her forehead.

'Your temperature's down. Could you manage a cup of tea?'

'Yes. I think perhaps I could.'

'I'll go and make one, but you have to promise me that you won't try and get up by yourself.'

'I promise. Jack?'

He turned in the doorway. 'Yes?'

'Thank you for staying.'

'Any time, Rosie.'

Why did he have to be so flippant? she thought crossly. Most men would have run a mile. 'Did anyone phone from the office?' she asked.

'If you're asking if Anthony rang,' he said, without expression, 'then I'm afraid the answer is no. Perhaps it's as well under the circumstances. I'm sure he extracted a promise from you never to see me again?'

'Is that what you would have done?'

He shook his head. 'No, sweetheart.

You'll stay with me because you want to. Not because of some unreal notion of security. Not because of a promise extracted when you're feeling anxious and guilty. You'll stay because you can't do anything else.' His words were shocking. Not because of the sentiment expressed, but because he obviously thought she couldn't do anything else. He had come to the flat expecting to be made welcome. She had to explain, convince him that he was wrong, but he didn't wait for her response. 'When Sarah phoned wanting you to take over some fresh clothes, I asked her to speak to Anthony.' He hesitated. 'She thought it was probably better if Anthony thought she was looking after you. She was going to suggest he stay away in case he caught your flu.'

He wouldn't need that kind of prompt. His mother would certainly tell him to stay away. 'I don't think he would need much persuading after yesterday . . . '

'Yesterday?' His face suddenly creased

in a smile. 'If by yesterday you mean Thursday, my love, I have to tell you that today is Sunday.'

'Sunday?' Her finely drawn brows drew together in the slightest frown. 'But it can't be Sunday.'

He walked across to the chair and handed her the newspaper. 'See for yourself. We all know they don't lie. At least not about the date.'

'But that means you've been here . . . ' It was too much effort to work out, but it must have been days. Where had he slept? But she was suddenly too tired to care. She lay back against the pillows.

'Yes, I've been here,' he said, tucking the quilt under her chin. 'Someone had to look after you. For an ambitious and well-motivated young woman you seem totally incapable of looking after your-self.'

'That's not true!' she declared, struggling up from the depths of her pillow, propping herself on an elbow. 'I never had the slightest problem until you came along. I've never lost my keys.

I've never been ill. I've never . . . ' She stopped. His face, the strong bones moulded by the shaded light of the lamp, was just above her. She wanted to reach up and smooth away the dark shadows beneath his eyes.

He brushed a curl back from her forehead. 'What else is it that you've never done, Rosie?'

Never fallen in love, she thought as he straightened and turned away, apparently not expecting an answer. She lay back. How could it have happened? Less than a week ago her life had been clearly mapped out. There hadn't been the slightest doubt in her mind that she was going to marry Anthony. For a while she would continue with her career, eventually they would have children. It was planned, orderly, with no room for unpleasant surprises. Jack Drayton was an irresponsible rogue. Charming, fun to be with. Not someone to fall in love with if you valued your peace of mind.

With the tea he brought a boiled egg

and a slice of bread and butter and put it on the bedside table. She regarded him from beneath the bedclothes.

'Can you sit up?' he asked. Then frowned. 'What's the matter?'

'Nothing.' She swallowed. Not true.

'Come on, I'll help.'

'No. It's all right.' She struggled into a sitting position. He continued to stare at her for a moment, then turned his attention to the tray.

'Let's see you try a little of this.' Despite her protests that she wasn't hungry, he insisted she try a little of the egg, holding the spoon to her lips until she obeyed him. In the end she managed to swallow most of it. Afterwards she demanded he let her up to wash.

'You're not strong enough.'

'Of course I am. I can't just lie here . . .' Her attempt to prove her strength by swinging her legs out of bed would have brought her to grief, but for Jack catching her as she pitched forward.

'Don't you ever learn, Rosie?' he demanded. 'Just lie there.'

'I feel disgusting,' she said, tetchy because she didn't want to cry. She never cried.

'Then we'll do something about it, but you're going to have to accept that you've been very ill.'

'It's just a touch of flu. I'll be fine tomorrow.'

'I think I preferred you when you had lost your voice.'

'I preferred you when you weren't here!'

'Well, Rosie, I have to agree that if your temper is any indication you appear to be on the mend,' he said. 'But I suggest you leave the prognosis to the doctor. I think you'll find he disagrees with you.'

'The doctor? You mustn't bother him. He'll be rushed off his feet.'

'He's been four times in three days. He's calling again in the morning. You don't want him to ring a peal about my ears for not looking after you

172

properly, do you?'

'Four times?' This did more than her own weak state to convince her that she had been really ill.

'Now will you lie back and behave yourself?' She nodded, too weak for further protest. 'Then I'll get a bowl of water and we'll see what we can do to make you feel better.'

She did as she was told, unable to raise more than the feeblest token of resistance when she realised he intended to wash her himself.

'I thought you were going to behave,' he chided her gently.

'You can't, Jack.'

'Stop me,' he invited, as he wrung out the flannel. She submitted to the indignity of having her face washed for the first time since she could reach a wash-basin for herself. He was brisk and businesslike about it and when he held her over his arm, pulled off her nightgown and washed her back it was done so impersonally that she knew it would be ridiculous to object when he did the same to her front. But she closed her eyes; at least that way she could pretend it wasn't happening. He slipped a clean nightdress over her head, helped with the arms, then left her to wriggle into it under the covers.

'Anything else?' he asked, when he came back a few moments later.

'Could you pass me my hairbrush?'

He picked up the silver-backed brush that had been her grandmother's, weighed it in his hand and then handed it to her without a word. She tried to lift it, then let it fall back to the bed. He took it from her and began to restore the tangled chestnut curls to some order.

'It needs washing,' she said, self-consciously as he stroked the brush through it.

'It'll keep,' he replied, a little brusquely. 'Right now I think you should go to sleep.'

Her lids were already half closed. Jack leaned over her and as she drifted off into sleep she thought his lips

174

brushed her forehead. But maybe she just dreamed it.

★ ★ ★

When she woke, it was Sarah leaning over her and she wondered if it had all been a dream.

'Hello, Rose. How're you doing?'

She tested her limbs, moved her head. 'I think I feel a little better.'

'The doctor's here. We'll see what he says.'

The doctor's verdict was much the same as her own. On the mend, but weak. 'You need at least a week of pampering, Miss Parry. Two weeks would be better, but I have no doubt you'll tell me that's impossible.'

'It's impossible.'

He grinned appreciatively. 'Definitely on the mend. You've your young man to thank for that.'

Not a dream, then. 'He's not . . . ' She decided not to try and explain. It was too complicated. 'Thank you for

175

coming out. You must be terribly busy.'

'The worst of the epidemic seems to be over, thank goodness.' He wrote out a sick note and left it beside the bed. 'This is for two weeks. Try and take it, Miss Parry.'

'I'll try,' she promised.

Sarah came back after seeing the doctor out and sat on the edge of the bed. 'What's the verdict?'

'He wants me to take two weeks' sick leave. How's Matt?'

'Much better. But he wasn't nearly as bad as you.'

She hesitated, unwilling to ask the obvious question, but wanting to know. 'Where's Jack?'

'Missing him already?'

She dismissed the question as ridiculous. 'Of course not. I just wanted to thank him. He was very kind.'

'Yes,' Sarah said, gravely, but her eyes sparkled with humour. 'He was very kind.' She relented. 'And he'll be back in an hour or two. He had an appointment that he couldn't cancel so he asked me to come back and keep an eye on you. So, shall we take advantage of his absence and get you into the bath?'

Bathed, her hair washed and dried by Sarah, she was propped up in bed with some breakfast when the doorbell rang. She looked up expectantly as the door opened but Sarah came back alone, carrying a single red rose.

'This I call style,' Sarah said, sniffing the bloom appreciatively.

There was no card. 'Who is it from?'

'Rosalind Parry! You're getting married in a couple of months. How can you ask such a question? I'll put it in water.'

The idea of Anthony sending a single rose was slightly unreal. His romance quotient was on the low side.

A little later the bell rang again. 'More flowers.' Sarah handed her the bouquet with slightly raised brows. Pink carnations and a card. 'Get well soon, love, Anthony'.

They both glanced at the single red

rose in the bud vase that Sarah had placed beside the bed and Rosalind found herself blushing.

'I'll go and find a vase,' Sarah said, quickly.

'Sarah!'

Sarah turned somewhat reluctantly to face her friend. 'What is it?'

She lay back, suddenly quite exhausted. 'Nothing.' Nothing that Sarah could help with. They both knew that.

'Don't worry about it now, Rose. Go back to sleep for a while. It'll all sort itself out.'

She closed her eyes, but sleep was more elusive. Her body was weak, but her mind seemed to race. Jack said she was paying a high price for security, but he didn't understand. No one understood, except perhaps her mother. She had known what it was like to be married to a man who always wanted to be somewhere else. Doing something else. Who hated to be tied to a house, responsibilities. Hated it so much that despite his love for her mother he had finally left them both. Put on his coat one day and simply walked away. Beguiled by the sound of a 'different drummer'. A tear rolled down Rose's cheek at the pain of his desertion. How could he have gone? Never writing, never phoning. Totally uncaring that the bottom had fallen out of her world with his disappearance.

Anthony would never do that. He was solid. Conventional. A marrying man. She had thought she longed for that kind of security, yet ever since Jack Drayton had crossed her path like a latter-day Pied Piper offering her untold wonders in the sound of a saxophone she too had been beguiled.

She sighed. She had always had a touch of her father's wildness in her. She had tried to crush it, heaven knew, but maybe she was more like him than she was prepared to admit. Until she was more sure of herself she could never marry Anthony. With that decision made, a load seemed to lift from her mind and she finally slept.

★ ★ ★

She stretched, languorously, and opened her eyes to find Jack smiling down at her.

'Hello,' she said, suddenly well enough to feel shy at this intimacy.

'How are you?'

'Much better. Thank you.'

'Could you eat something? Sarah made some chicken soup before she left.'

'Left?'

'She's gone back to Matt's. She said you'd understand. Rosie, is your mother away? I've been trying to get her all weekend.'

'Have you?' For a moment she couldn't think why he would want to speak to her mother. Then the penny dropped. He wanted her to come and take over. He'd had enough of playing nursemaid. 'I'm sorry, Jack. I must have been a dreadful nuisance to you.'

'Dreadful,' he agreed, earnestly. 'And in your weakened state I haven't been able to take advantage of the situation, which is a pity. But, Sarah's going back to work tomorrow and I have some business that I just can't put off any longer.'

'You really don't have to worry about me any more. I'll be fine now,' she said, stiffly, not wanting to think about the business he had in mind.

'If I want to worry about you, I will. I asked about your mother.'

'What date is it? Mum was going away some time before Easter. I can't remember when, exactly. She was taking some of the older children to London for a few days.'

'Older children?'

'She's head teacher in a primary school.'

'Well, I've left a message on her answering machine. I imagine she'll phone as soon as she gets back. I thought you might stay with her for few days until you've quite recovered — '

'That won't be necessary. I'm going back to work — '

'Not this week, even if I have to cancel all my meetings. Not next week if I can help it, but I've no doubt that by then you'll be strong enough to tell me to go to hell.'

Meetings! Was that the word they used? 'I should have done that the moment I set eyes on you,' she said, with a good deal of feeling.

'Hmm. Well, have a bowl of soup first.'

'Only if I can sit at the table. I feel welded to this bed.'

'You sound stronger with every word.' He held out a dressing-gown and she fed her arms into it, then rose slowly to her feet. She swayed slightly and he held her. 'All right?'

She looked up into his face. 'Fine.' His expression altered imperceptibly from concern to something deeper, more intense. She was suddenly very conscious that she was leaning against him wearing a flimsy nightdress, that they were alone and for days he had looked after her in the most intimate way. The sudden heat that seared her cheeks had nothing to do with influenza.

She dropped her eyes and began to fumble with the buttons of her dressing-gown, but Jack caught her wrist and stopped her. 'Better let me do that; you've got them all wrong.' He fastened each one with careful precision and led her through to the kitchen and sat her down at the table.

'Why did you stay, Jack?' she asked, as she watched him pour soup into a bowl.

He made an impatient gesture. 'Why do you always want to analyse everything, Rosie? Let's just say it was convenient. I had nowhere else more important to go.'

'Oh, I see.' He had cared for her in return for helping himself to her sofa.

'I very much doubt it, Rosie. Just eat your soup.' She ate a few spoonfuls, then left her spoon in the bowl. 'That's not enough. Finish it, or it's straight back to bed with you.' She glared at him but eventually managed most of it and he relented and settled her in the armchair by the fire before clearing up.

The phone began to ring. She knew from experience that he was unlikely to hear it in the kitchen, so she struggled to her feet and answered it herself.

'Rosalind? Is that you?'

She leaned weakly against the wall. 'Hello, Anthony. Thank you for the flowers.'

'Flowers . . . ? Oh, Julie thought you would like them. You sound terrible.'

Good old Julie, she might have known. 'Thanks.'

'I'm sorry, I didn't mean — '

'It's all right, Anthony. I know I sound terrible. How are you coping?'

On the safer ground of work, Anthony was effusive. 'Very well. Quite a few people had recovered enough to get in today and Julie's sister was a great help over the weekend.'

'She's a nice girl. We could do worse than offer her a job when she leaves school.' A spasm of coughing caught her and she paused for breath. 'How are you? No sign of succumbing?'

'No, thank goodness. Mother has been working herself into such a state. I don't know what I would have done if Julie hadn't very kindly done some shopping for her on Saturday afternoon.'

Rosalind felt the unspoken criticism. Anthony had thrown out a good many hints in her direction about doing his mother's shopping during the flu outbreak. She had studiously ignored every one of them.

'Julie's a very kind person.'

'Mother asked her to stay to supper.' He cleared his throat. 'She had expected you, so it was no bother,' he added, in case she worried that Mrs Harlowe had been put to any trouble.

'Well, that was . . . nice.' She wondered what on earth she was doing standing in a chilly hall having a conversation about Julie. 'Who looked after her children?' she asked. There was a catch of something in her voice, but Anthony didn't seem to notice.

'Oh, she brought them with her. Beautifully behaved little girls. Mother was very taken by them. I always thought Julie was divorced, you know, I hadn't realised she was a widow.'

'Anthony, I must go. It's cold in the hall.'

'Oh, I'm sorry. I just wondered if there was anything we could get for you? Julie offered — '

Julie again? 'No, Anthony. I don't want anything. I . . . I think I'll go and stay with my mother for a few days. I'll ring you from there.' She put the phone down and turned to find Jack watching her from the doorway. 'You can't hear the phone from the kitchen,' she said, guiltily.

'Come back to the fire. You're shivering.' He slipped his arm around her and she leaned gratefully against his shoulder.

'The wind seems to howl under that door.' She shuddered convulsively. 'It's a very effective way of keeping down the phone bills.'

He put a mug of hot chocolate into her hand. 'Drink this and then I think perhaps you should go back to bed. You've been up for long enough.'

She nodded and sipped the drink. 'Jack?'

'Yes?'

'I've decided to go and stay with mother for a few days. If it will help, you can stop here for a few more days.'

'You've changed your mind about leaving me to the tender mercies of the Salvation Army, then?' He squatted down in front of her, blue questing eyes searching her face. 'What about Anthony?' he asked. 'Won't he object?'

She shrugged, awkwardly. 'He needn't know.'

'And if I insisted you tell him?' he asked.

'I . . . ' She faltered, not ready to betray feelings that were too new, too tender to stand close scrutiny. Her eyes begged him to understand.

He touched her cheek, very gently, with the tips of his fingers. 'Thank you for the offer, Rosie. But I'm afraid I've never been interested in fifty per cent of anything.'

7

The sudden peal of the doorbell prevented Rosalind from flinging herself into his arms and making a complete idiot of herself.

For a moment Jack stayed there, almost as if he hoped she might still commit herself. Then he stood up and went to answer the door. Her mother burst into the room, bringing with her a taste of cold air and a fit of scolding.

'Why on earth didn't you have your flu shot, Rosalind?' she began, without preamble. 'I reminded you at the beginning of the winter.'

'Hello, Mum.'

Mrs Parry turned to Jack. 'She hates needles. I should have known she wouldn't do it unless I came and held her hand.' Then she frowned. 'I don't think I know you. Are you a neighbour?'

He glanced at Rose. 'I live . . . nearby,' he agreed. 'I left a message on your answering machine.' He held out his hand. 'Jack Drayton.'

'Jane Parry.' She took his hand. 'Thank you for letting me know that Rosalind was ill.' She looked back at her daughter and tutted. 'Into bed with you. You look like a damp rag.'

Rose and Jack exchanged a glance. 'I'll be going, Rosie, now your mother's here.'

'Jack, wait. There's no need . . . '

'I suppose Anthony's at home, coddling his hypochondriac of a mother,' Mrs Parry, carried on, sweeping her daughter towards the bedroom. Rose looked back helplessly and her mother followed her glance. 'Goodbye, Mr Drayton.'

Rosalind was not quite certain what made her angrier, her mother taking over in her high school-mistress style, or Jack trying very hard not to laugh as she was frog-marched back to bed.

'Goodbye, Rosie,' he raised his hand in salute as her mother's hand in the small of her back propelled her firmly towards the bedroom. 'Look after yourself.' And you, Jack, she said silently. Look after yourself. She was in bed with a thermometer in her mouth when she heard the outside door close with its customary rattle. She had never thanked him for the rose.

'This isn't necessary,' she mumbled. 'I'm much better.'

'Be quiet for a minute.' Her mother whisked her flowers out of the bedroom while she waited for her temperature to register. When she came back she took the thermometer, tutted again and tucked the quilt around Rose's shoulders. 'I'll take you home with me tomorrow. I can't stay away from school, but I can at least keep an eye on you there.' She gave her daughter a hard look. 'You obviously need keeping an eye on,' she said, with meaning.

'Mum, I'm not a little girl — '

Her mother patted the bedclothes. 'Just go to sleep, Rosalind. You can tell me all about it when you're feeling better.'

All about what? There was nothing to tell.

* * *

When she had been home for nearly a week Rosalind began to get restless. She was unused to idleness and found so much of it tedious. She wandered about the house, forbidden to do any housework or cooking by her mother. She had read anything that looked remotely interesting and there was nothing on the television.

She lifted the lid of the piano and let the fingers of one hand run over the keys. Her mother kept it tuned, which surprised her. No one had played it properly since her father left. She sat down and began to pick out a tune, gradually losing herself in her pleasure at rediscovering a small talent. She had been playing for a while when she became gradually aware of an over-laying sound. She stopped. There was a

192

sharp tapping at the window and she looked around.

'Jack!' He was at the french windows and she flew to let him in.

'I couldn't make anyone hear me at the door, but I heard the piano.' He peered around the door. 'Is the headmistress home?'

She shook her head. 'You're quite safe, Jack. She's still at school.' She was suddenly awkward and found it easier to be busy shutting the door, easier to look at her feet. 'It's good to see you.'

'Is it?' He tipped her chin upwards. 'We'll see. I have a feeling you would be pleased to see anyone after a week of your mother.'

'Jack!' Then quite unexpectedly, she giggled. 'You mustn't take it personally. She treats everyone like a five-year-old. I think being a headteacher has something to do with it.'

He had wandered over to the piano and ran his hand over the keys. 'Is that why your father left?' he asked, glancing up at her.

'No!' Her forehead creased in a frown at this unexpected reminder of that betrayal. 'No, of course not. He left because . . . well, playing the piano was in the end more important to him than either of us.'

'She could have gone with him. Some women do, you know.' He sat down on the stool and began to pick out the tune she had been playing. 'But perhaps — when he asked her to make a choice — her home and job were more important than he was?'

'You know nothing about it, Jack.'

'Do you?'

The question was a shock. No one had ever suggested that the decision to part had been anything but her father's. Rich Parry had wanted more than a quiet life in a small rural town and so he had left home and hearth for the bright lights. Jack stopped playing and turned to her. 'How did that part of the tune go?' She hesitated only for a moment, then moved beside him and played a few notes. 'It's pretty.'

'Dada wrote it for me. Years ago. He'd try anything to get me to practise.'

'I'd like to learn it. Sit down here and let me follow you.'

She and her father had regularly shared the long piano stool, so she sat beside him and played the notes and he echoed her until finally they finished the tune with a boisterous crescendo. 'You knew it all along,' she accused, laughing, as the sound died away.

'Yes,' he admitted. 'But wasn't it a good way of getting you this close?' She made a move to rise, but his arm was around her before she could escape. 'Are you really pleased to see me, Rosie?' he demanded.

To say how pleased she was meant total exposure and she had never given that much of herself to anyone. This wasn't ever going to be like the civilised arrangement she had with Anthony. If she gave Jack the hundred per cent he demanded from her, there would be nothing left for anyone else. Ever. A basic need to preserve a part of herself

195

held her back. 'Well, Jack,' she said, 'as you said, anyone would have been a welcome distraction . . . '

'Anyone?' He tilted his head slightly, regarding her from beneath lids that shaded his amusement.

'Anyone,' she confirmed, raising her chin defiantly. He took shameless advantage of this tactical error, bending swiftly to caress the hollow of her throat with warm lips. She shivered as liquid pleasure fired through her veins and his hands slid across her back, pulling her closer into the circle of his arms until she was pressed close against his chest and could feel the steady thud of his heartbeat against her breast. 'Anyone?' he murmured.

'Jack . . . ' Her protest died away as his mouth began to tease the delicate skin beneath her chin, the line of her jaw, then his teeth grazed her earlobe and she shuddered and tried to pull free.

'Answer me, Rosie.'

'I . . . ' Her throat was constricted.

She wanted to tell him she had been waiting, hoping every day that he would ring. That the sudden sight of him had evoked a joy so special that for a moment she had been unable to believe it.

'You seem to have lost your voice again, Rosie. Why don't you just show me?' The words grated over her skin, raising a prickle of excitement that tingled along her spine and made her catch her breath.

For a long moment she remained motionless in his arms. She could kiss him. Heaven knew how much she longed to, but he was demanding far more than that. A hundred per cent. She wondered briefly if he knew what he was asking of her. She knew. She had no illusions that life would, could ever be the same. The prospect of her career, a safe marriage, two point four children at decent intervals would be lost forever. Wrapped in the circle of Jack's arms, she almost didn't care. But if she surrendered to him she knew she would go anywhere, do anything he wanted. She wouldn't make the same mistake her mother had and demand that he change for her and she still didn't know whether she was capable of that amount of giving.

But her arms seemed to know what they wanted, even if her head did not. They slid up the soft wool of his sweater and entwined themselves around his neck. He made no move to help her. A hundred per cent. Everything. She swayed towards him, offering her softly parted lips to this raider of her heart. Still he waited, wanting more. Something about that total self-control fired her, kindled an explosive challenge that she rose to as helplessly as a salmon to an angler's lure.

Shamelessly she ran the tip of her tongue along his lower lip, probing gently, begging admittance and she felt a kind of exhilaration as the tension bit into the muscles under the smooth skin of his neck. Surer now of her power, her demand that he respond to her was suddenly imperative. She wanted him and she showed it in the way she held herself against him, the way her fingers drew him down to her, in a kiss that answered every question he cared to ask of her. And then quite unexpectedly she found the situation reversed.

He was in control and it was she who was submerged beneath the shattering impact of his kiss. His hand slid over her body to caress her breast, the nipple that tightened to the touch of his fingers. His tongue stroked along hers, sweet and urgent until she thought, hoped, that the world would end before they parted. When finally, he drew back, she cried out and clung to him.

'Jack, I want — ' His fingers on her lips stopped the words.

'Good afternoon, Mrs Parry.'

Rose swung round. Her mother was standing in the doorway regarding her daughter with a slightly puzzled expression. 'Mum, I can explain . . . '

'There is nothing to explain, Rosalind. I'm not so old that I can't remember the details for myself. It's Mr Drayton, isn't it?'

He stood up. 'Yes, although I'd rather you called me Jack.'

Her look was not encouraging. 'Perhaps you would care to make yourself comfortable over there, Mr Drayton. You seem a little cramped on the piano stool.'

'We were playing . . . '

'The piano? Are you a musician, Mr Drayton? You certainly seem to know all the right notes to play.' There was almost a look of despair in the glance she threw her daughter. 'Have you invited Mr Drayton to dinner, Rosalind?' she asked.

'No,' Jack interjected. 'I was just passing through and I stopped to see how Rosie was.'

'Clearly she has been able to demonstrate how well she has recovered. I'll see you out.'

'Mum, stop it!' Rose finally found her

voice. 'How dare you be so rude?' Her mother's raised eyebrows, honed on generations of cheeky little boys, nearly stopped her in her tracks. But she had started something that needed to be said and it was too late to back away from it. 'I'm not five years old, Mum.'

'So I noticed.' She threw a look at Jack. 'I was simply thinking of Anthony.'

'I know. But it's really none of your business. Jack is my guest, a friend. Perhaps more.' She felt her cheeks burn. 'It's too soon to say. But if you had a lover I wouldn't be so ill-mannered as to remind you that you're still married to Dad.'

'Rosalind! That's enough!'

'I'm sorry if that offends you. I'm not sorry that I said it.'

'Since I still love your father the situation isn't likely to arise.' She smiled a little wryly at her daughter's shocked expression. 'Sit down, Jack. Wherever you like. I'll go and make some tea.'

'No. Thank you, Mrs Parry,' he said,

gently. 'I really do have to go.'

'Then I'll leave you to say goodbye to Rosalind.'

'Goodbye, Mrs Parry.' She nodded and closed the door on the way out. 'Do you think she meant that?' Jack asked, as he took Rose into his arms. 'About still loving your father?'

'She never says anything she doesn't mean,' she said, still stunned by her mother's declaration.

'And you?' he insisted. 'Do you sometimes say things you don't mean? What about that promise to Anthony?'

'I meant everything I said today,' she said, still evading a direct answer. 'Couldn't you tell?'

'If you're asking for marks out of ten, Rosie, I could tell you were trying hard. Very hard.' Her face flamed and she tried desperately to pull away, but he held her effortlessly pinned to his chest, his expression fierce, his voice harsh. 'When you give a hundred per cent, Rosie, you don't have to ask. You know.'

His mouth claimed hers briefly and

then he was gone. She was still holding on to the piano for support, still trying to regain her breath, when her mother brought in the tea tray.

* * *

She returned to work on Wednesday. Anthony was surprised to see her. Shocked almost, she thought. She had made a special effort with her make-up and thought she looked quite well, but perhaps she was fooling herself.

'Are you sure you should be back, Rosalind?' he asked, anxiously, and guilt at his concern made things worse. 'We can manage for a few more days, you know . . . '

'Yes, I can see. You seem to have managed remarkably well,' she said.

'Well, Julie has been wonderful.'

'Yes, she's very supportive. Anthony, we have to talk about the wedding arrangements.'

'Do we?' He shifted in his seat.

'Yes, I'm afraid we do.'

'Not in the office.'

No. Not in the office. Hardly the place to tell a man you've known for years that you've decided that you can't marry him after all.

'Can you come round this evening? After work?'

'No. I've a partners' dinner tonight at the Napier Hotel.'

'Anthony, this won't wait.' She had to tell him. Get it off her chest. If she never saw Jack Drayton again, she knew she could never marry Anthony and she had to explain. It was only fair.

'Won't it?' He seemed edgy. 'Well, you can meet me for a drink in the bar at about seven o'clock?'

Neutral territory? Perhaps that would be a good thing. And afterwards there would be the dinner to keep his mind occupied.

'Yes, of course.'

She returned to her own little office space. Julie too was edgy. 'We've made a couple of sales while you've been away,' she said, almost defensively.

'Fine, Julie. You've done wonderfully. Anthony is very pleased with you.'

The woman blushed. 'The Lodge at Wickham has been sold.'

'Wickham Lodge?' She made an effort at a smile. 'I rather liked the place myself.'

'Yes.' There was something in the woman's tone that made Rosalind look up and frown. Almost as if she knew. But surely Anthony would never have told her? 'You said, when you went to look the place over,' she added.

'Did I?' She didn't remember. 'Well, perhaps you'd better walk me through the rest of what's been happening while I've been on my sick bed.'

The day had been quiet enough, yet she felt completely drained when she let herself into her apartment that evening and she still had to face Anthony.

She made a special effort to dress in the way he liked. It seemed the least she could do. A simple black dress, her hair in a sleek chignon. She picked up the watch from the dressing-table and put it back into its box. She would give it back to him. It was impossible to keep it under the circumstances.

It was just before seven when she parked in the Napier's vast car park and went through into the bar. Anthony was already waiting in the corner seat and rose as she joined him.

He took her hands and bent to kiss her cheek. The gesture was so unexpected, so spontaneous that it took her by surprise.

'Can I get you something to drink, Rosalind?'

She shook her head. 'No, thank you.'

'Sit down.' He sat facing her for a moment before he began to speak. 'I have something to tell you, Rosalind. I'm not sure how to begin.'

He was so grave that her heart began to beat anxiously. She tried to cover her anxiety under a joke. 'Whatever's the matter? Are the partners bankrupt?'

'No, my dear. Your job is safe. In fact, I think after this evening you'll find your position improved. It's not work I wish to talk to you about.' This was not how she had imagined it at all. She had rehearsed exactly what she would say. How she would take the blame entirely. But it was all getting away from her and she had to seize the initiative before she lost her nerve. She placed the jeweller's box containing the gold watch upon the table and pushed it towards him. He frowned. 'What is this?'

'I'm returning the watch you gave me for my birthday, Anthony.' She didn't wait for him to ask why. 'I can't marry you.' She had expected him to be angry. Bluster a little. But he just looked at her as if he couldn't believe his ears. 'I'm sorry.'

'Who told you?' he demanded.

'Told me what?'

'Rosalind, I can quite understand that you would want to make the break yourself. I thank you for it. It makes it easier for me. But that you should have found out from someone else — '

'I'm sorry, Anthony,' she interrupted

him. 'I have no idea what you're talking about.'

'Julie. Julie and me.'

The penny dropped. Julie's strange manner. 'You and Julie? Isn't that rather sudden, Anthony.'

He smiled. 'Mind-numbingly sudden. Quite wonderful.' He was suddenly all concern. 'I'm sorry. I hoped you'd understand.'

'Oh, I understand, my dear friend. I do understand.' She leaned across and placed her hand on his. 'I hope you'll be very happy.'

'What about you? Will that saxophone player make you happy?'

'I don't know. I'm not even sure if I'll see him again.' She straightened. 'You'd better go to your dinner, or you'll be late.'

'Yes, I suppose so.' He picked up the box and opened it. 'This is your birthday present, Rosalind. Please don't give it back.'

'Julie — '

'I gave you this before I realised she

existed.' He took it out and fastened it around her wrist. 'A present from a friend. I hope we can still be friends?'

She didn't want to take the watch back, but sensed that he needed to feel she had forgiven him. She leaned across and kissed his cheek. 'Thank you, Anthony. Be happy.' She walked quickly away, not looking back, determined that he shouldn't see the sting of tears in her eyes and mistake them for regret. Her only regret was that she had been too cowardly to take something special with both hands when it was offered. Everything had seemed too much to give. Now it seemed too little.

She made it to the powder room, determined to regain her composure, put a brave face on before she confronted the lobby. She freshened her lipstick and realised the girl next to her was smiling through the mirror. 'You were at the jazz club the other night with Jack, weren't you?' the girl said.

Rosalind nodded uncertainly. 'Yes.'

Then she remembered. 'Of course, you were the singer. You're very good.'

The girl's smile broadened in appreciation. 'Thank you. Jack's been such a help. He said I was singing the wrong material.'

'He's been playing at the club?'

The girl smiled. 'Playing . . . ? Oh, no. Are you here for the party?'

'Party?'

'He's throwing a party to celebrate taking over. Mike was pretty desperate, you know. On the point of bankruptcy. They were actually thinking of turning the place into a snooker club.'

'I remember. He said something about it.'

'He's given me a contract,' the girl added, confidentially.

'Mike?'

'No. Mike's gone. Jack's taken the place over, having it all done up. I thought you would have known.'

There was a cold spot in the pit of her stomach. 'No. I didn't know. Congratulations,' she said. 'I'm sure you deserve it.'

'He's bringing in a new manager and a lot of first class musicians so things should improve.' The girl outlined her lips in a vivid red. 'Of course he's got the money to keep things going. Mike told me it's more of a hobby with him. Like playing the sax.'

The cold feeling was spreading. Small icy fingers that crept along her veins, finding every hidden corner to touch and chill. 'He has money?'

'I thought you knew him? After all — '

'We're just acquaintances.'

'Oh.' She shrugged. 'Well, he's one of those computer wizards. Apparently he'd made a fortune by the time he was twenty and doubled it every year since.'

'Then why is he in Melchester?' Rosalind asked, a little sharply. 'It's hardly a millionaires' playground.'

The girl turned and looked directly at her. 'Do you know, that's exactly what I said! But he had some personal business here and liked the place. He's been staying at a friend's house out at Wickham and now he's decided to buy it.' She shrugged. 'But I suppose it's only a country cottage for the likes of him.'

'I suppose so.' And meanwhile he had been amusing himself at the expense of the yokels to while away the time in between deals.

They walked out into the reception area together. 'Why don't you come in and say hello to everyone? It's very informal. I'm sure Jack would be pleased to see you.'

'Do you think so?' The board listing the functions for the evening of the first of March showed Drayton Enterprises in the Wellington Room. Drayton Enterprises. There could be no mistake. 'Why is Jack holding a party here, with the club at his disposal?'

'He's having it redecorated.' She paused in the doorway and looked back. 'Are you coming in?'

'In a minute. You go on.' Rosalind stood in the doorway and looked around. It was a moment before she saw him, seated quietly in a corner talking to a couple of men. The dinner-jacket clung to his shoulders exactly as she had known it would. She had recognised the quality but, blinded by whatever game he was playing with her, she had not seen the truth.

He hadn't been trespassing in the house. The car was his. He had never denied it, choosing instead to allow her to make a fool of herself. And she had certainly done that. Why he had come into her office and played to her, kissed her, she didn't understand. What he hoped to gain by his deception, she had no idea. She only knew that she felt utterly betrayed and as she stood there watching him, relaxed, perfectly at home in these opulent surroundings, the ice in her veins turned to fire.

She edged her way through the crowded room, was spoken to by people who recognised her and she replied briefly, but didn't halt.

'Can I help you, madam?' The chef at

the buffet table began to tempt her from the rich display of food. 'If you'd like to take a plate?'

'Thank you.' She considered for a moment the delicacies spread out before her. Finally, her eye alighted on a long silver platter containing a salmon mousse, as yet untouched, beautifully decorated with fine scales of cucumber and recumbent in a sea of lettuce and she smiled. 'I'll take this.' She picked up the dish and began to move away from the table.

'Er, no . . . madam. I'll serve you.'

'It's all right, it's for Mr Drayton,' she said, reassuringly. 'I'll see to it myself.' She didn't wait for the man's response, but headed towards the corner.

He had his back to her and didn't see her coming. The polite enquiring smiles of his companions alerted him to the fact that there was someone behind him and he turned, glanced up, registered her presence with obvious surprise and quickly rose to his feet.

'Rosie, how lovely to see you.' She admired the aplomb with which he had recovered his poise. No one could possibly have told from his bearing that he had just received a severe jolt.

'Hello, Jack.'

'When did you get home?' he asked, with every sign of pleasure at seeing her, as he pulled back a chair. 'Come and sit down.'

She shook her head. 'No thanks. I'm not staying.' She smiled at the two other occupants at the table. 'I'm gate-crashing,' she added, confidentially. 'I'm not supposed to be here.'

'Don't be silly, sweetheart.' There was a warning edge to his voice. 'Let me take that — '

'Silly?' She raised her eyebrows in mock surprise. 'I'm not being silly, Jack,' she assured him, moving the dish out of his reach. 'But when I discovered you were having a party, I just had to come and say how much I admired the enormous strides you've made in the last couple of weeks.' She referred back to their fascinated audience. 'Did you know that only two weeks ago, Mr Drayton was earning a few pounds doing kiss-o-grams in his spare time?' She allowed this interesting fact to sink in. 'Possibly a little more than that. Have you seen the Ferrari?' The two men exchanged a glance and Jack's face darkened, dangerously. 'And he was squatting in an empty house? Now look.' They ducked nervously as strips of lettuce parted company with the salmon as she swung it in a careless arc at the crowded room. 'Buying a jazz club, throwing a party at the Napier. Quite the most remarkable upturn in his fortunes wouldn't you say? Is he giving you tips on how to do it?' she asked.

'Rosie!' he warned.

She shook her head. 'It's quite simple,' she advised her fascinated listeners in a tone of the utmost confidentiality. 'I can tell you exactly how he does it. He gives everything a hundred per cent effort,' she continued, as if he hadn't spoken. 'That must be the secret of his success, wouldn't you think? No half-measures. All or nothing.'

8

Jack rocked back on his heels as the salmon mousse began to accelerate on its return journey, anticipating the moment of contact and easily avoiding it. But the heavy chilled dish had dewed with moisture and as Rosalind swung at him, intending merely to splatter him, humiliate him as she felt humiliated, it flew from her hand. The ornate sculptured edge connected sharply with his face, catching his cheek bone with a sickening crunch, snapping back his head, knocking him sideways so that only the wall prevented him from crashing to the floor. The brightness of his blood from the gash on his cheek mingled in shocking contrast with the paler pink of the salmon that had smeared his face before splattering with spectacular success across the front of his jacket.

'You were right, Jack,' she said, into the sudden, shocking silence. 'When you give one hundred per cent there are no questions left to ask. No doubts. You should try it some time.'

She turned and walked quickly away from him, the stunned and silent crowd parting to let her through. 'Rosie! Come back damn you!' His voice bellowed across the room like the roar of an angry bull. It hammered against her like a blow, shivering her bones. Demanding, threatening, pleading almost. Blowing away the red haze of her temper.

She staggered slightly as the reality of what she had done hit her. She turned back, registered for the first time that he was hurt, saw him angrily shake off a helping hand and lurch towards her. She put up an arm as if to fend him off, but it was caught and held by someone close.

'Still got a temper then, *cariad*?' The voice was soft as a shawl of mist around the shoulders of Carreg Cennen. Welsh as the daffodil attached to his lapel for

St David. She registered the shock of hair, no longer carrot-bright, faded, streaked with silver now, the laughing green eyes, the nose battered by too many fierce encounters on a rugby field.

'Dada?' she whispered, hardly able to believe her eyes. He simply held out his arms and she fell gratefully into them. 'Take me home, Dada,' she begged. 'Please take me home.'

He glanced over her shoulder and pulled a face. 'Yes, I think that might be a wise move,' he said. 'Unless you're ready for round two? Jack doesn't look in the mood for a polite discussion. No, don't look back. Come with me. Now.' He moved her away from the reception room and out into the sharp night air. 'Have you got a car with you, Rosie?' he asked, moving swiftly away from the doorway and the fierce sound of an altercation behind them. He glanced at her, a glint of humour lighting his eyes. 'Or are we going to have to run for it?'

'Over there.' Her heart was hammering painfully and she began to shake as reaction to her outburst set in. 'But I don't think I can drive.'

'Perhaps not,' he said, opening the passenger door for her. 'But you'll have to give me some directions. They seem to have made everything one-way since I was last in Melchester.'

She told him the way, staring at him all the time, almost afraid that he was a figment of her imagination, conjured up by some genie out of the intensity of her need and that he might disappear if she took her eyes off him for a second. As he had disappeared once before.

'Where did you come from?' she asked. 'Where have you been?' The other question, the important question, Why did you leave me?, she didn't dare to ask.

'London today,' he said. 'America two days ago. I've spent the last month in New Orleans. You'd love it there, Rosie. The music! Oh, lord, the music.' He grinned at her and for a second it was as if he had never been away. But he had. He had simply packed his bags and gone. She withdrew slightly.

'Why didn't you ever write?'

He glanced across at her and frowned. 'But I did, *cariad*. A dozen times at least. Asking your mother to reconsider, come to me. I even sent the tickets.' He sighed. 'She never read the letters or cashed the cheques. She sent them all back unopened.'

Stunned, Rosalind sank back against her seat. 'I didn't know. She never said a word. I thought you had simply abandoned us.'

He pulled up outside the flat. 'A proud woman, your mother. I wanted her to come with me. Begged her to. You were on the point of leaving home for university, were starting a life of your own, but it made no difference. When we married I promised her I would forget about performing and take a teaching job. She wasn't about to change her life to follow a tramp's life following me about.'

'But you went anyway?'

'I had to. I was getting old and I hadn't done any of the things I'd promised myself.' He sighed. 'The sort of things you should do before you get married, I suppose.'

'And did you do them?' she asked, a little sharply. 'Did you enjoy yourself?'

His look begged understanding. 'Yes, *cariad*. Most of them anyway. But whether it was worth the loss is something I haven't come to terms with.'

'Self-discovery is painful?' she asked.

'I think perhaps you're in the throes of learning just how painful.' He looked at her, thoughtfully. 'But you're a little grown up these days for me to ask exactly what Jack did to deserve such cavalier treatment. And maybe I don't have the right.'

'Nothing to oil the shotgun for, Dada,' she reassured him. 'He allowed me to make a complete and utter fool of myself over him. No permanent harm done except to my pride,' she lied. She lifted her shoulders in a helpless little gesture that betrayed her feelings despite her brave words.

He patted her hand. 'Sometimes pride is all we've got, child. And as for making a fool of yourself . . . we're none of us immune from that particular bug. Are you going to invite me in? You can make me some coffee and tell me all your news.'

Her hesitation was only momentary. 'Yes, of course.'

She told him, at first a little grudgingly, about her job, about Anthony. Then about how she had met Jack and he laughed. 'It wasn't funny,' she scolded. Then quite spoilt the effect by giggling. 'You obviously know Jack Drayton,' she said. 'How did you meet him? No, wait. Don't tell me. I can guess. At a jazz club.'

'Where else? It was a few weeks ago, just after I arrived in New Orleans. He came to the club where I was playing, came backstage afterwards. We had a drink together, talked about home. I asked him to do an old man a favour and wish you a happy birthday from your Dada.'

'*You* asked . . . ?' Totally confused she went on. 'I thought he was a kiss-o-gram from the girls at the office. They never denied it . . . Oh, damn.' Her father's eyebrows shot up at this imprecation. 'Sorry. It's just he never said who the message was from . . . ' She thought about it. 'Maybe he didn't get a chance. At least, not then.' But Jack had asked about her family. And he had wanted to know if her mother was serious about still loving her father. Had he known then that Rich Parry was on his way home?

'I had a phone call from him at the weekend asking me if I'd like a job running the jazz club in Melchester, so I said I'd come and talk about it.' He grinned. 'Of course, he might be having second thoughts right now.'

'Oh, Dada, I'm sorry.'

'Don't be, *cariad*. If the pain was that bad, it was better to let it out. And if he isn't a big enough man to know he deserved it, then I wouldn't want to work for him.'

'But it's such a wonderful opportunity. Something you want to do, right here close to home . . . '

'Yes.' He hesitated. 'How close do you think your mother will let me get to it?'

'You do want to see her?'

'I didn't want to leave her, Rosie. I just couldn't stay as things were. And I'll tell you now that I won't go back to teaching the piano to children who would rather be playing some computer game. Do you think she would even talk to me on that basis?'

'Oh, yes, she said . . . ' She caught herself.

He was suddenly tense. 'What did she say?'

Rosie didn't tell him. What her mother had said was for her mother to repeat when she was good and ready. 'Just go and see her. Don't ring. Don't give her the chance to put on her armour.'

He laughed. 'You think I should steal up on her and take her by surprise?'

'It might work.' She smiled a little, remembering how Jack had done just that. 'The doorbell isn't working. If you don't get an answer, try the french window,' she advised.

His glance was penetrating. 'I'll bear that in mind. Now I'd better get back to the hotel before they lock me out. That is if they'll let me in at all. I may be wanted as an accessory on a charge of assault.'

'Dada! He wouldn't!'

'I think you could probably answer that question better than me.' She shook her head and buried her face in his shoulder to hide the sudden sting of tears as he held her. 'Can you ever forgive me for going away, Rosie?'

'I . . . I'm just glad you're back.'

And she was. But it wasn't enough to prevent the emptiness rushing back the minute he had gone. She was still weak from the flu virus and the evening had drained her emotionally. In the space of an hour she had lost the man she had planned to marry for as long as she could remember. And the man she had fallen in love with at the touch of his lips on hers. A flash-point, he had called it. A moment at which violent trouble began. He had been right about that at any rate.

Right now, all that was left was to put the pieces of her life back together and carry on as best she could. Perhaps she would follow her father's example and shake the dust of Melchester off her heels for a while. See a little of the world. It didn't really sound that much fun.

But the next day, she was sure that was what she must do. Julie had approached her diffidently, clearly expecting a rebuff. But she had no quarrel with Julie. She was certain she would make Anthony an excellent wife. She would not resent Mrs Harlowe, or living in the big house in the suburbs. She had had her romance. She had been widowed young and had a hard time bringing up two little girls on her own. Now she was settling for comfort and security. Exactly what Jack had accused her of.

Yet there was a glow about her and when Anthony came in later, he dropped a kiss on her cheek so easily and Julie had turned to him and said something that made him laugh. Something caught in her throat. They were in love.

'I hope you'll be happy, Julie,' she said. 'I hope you both will.' She found she meant it, sincerely.

'Will you come to the wedding, Rose?' she asked. 'It'll be a small affair. We aren't waiting.' She coloured. 'There doesn't seem any point.'

'Julie, surely you don't want me . . . '

'It would make us both happy. And you'll be working with Anthony. If you come, people will know that there are no hard feelings.'

Rose hesitated. She knew she had made up her own mind about Anthony, but they had been a couple for a long time and there was bound to be gossip.

She had no wish to go to the wedding in her present hollow mood, but Julie had a point. 'I'll come if you really want me to. When is the big day?'

'A week on Tuesday. I hope you can cope with the short notice?'

Rose managed to hide her surprise at the speed of things. 'We'll manage.' She had planned to leave as soon as possible, but in these circumstances it would not be so easy. Julie knew almost as much as she did about running the branch. If they both went it would cause a major problem.

The bell on the front office door rang and Julie went to deal with the enquiry. She came back a moment later. 'A gentleman with instructions for a country house, Rose. He asked for you.'

'Show him in here.' She reached for a pad and pen and when she looked up Jack was standing in front of her desk staring at a photograph of Wickham Lodge with its newly acquired 'SOLD' sticker. When he turned to face her, her hands flew to her mouth as she saw the stitches, the vivid bruise that darkened his cheekbone.

'Well?' he asked. 'Are you pleased with your handiwork?'

'I'm sorry. I didn't mean . . . '

He sank into the chair in front of her desk. 'Wrong answer, Rose. I asked for a hundred per cent and you certainly gave it that. For once in your life you did something you meant without holding anything back, without considering the consequences.'

Any guilt for the injury she had inflicted evaporated as he spoke. So he thought he'd won and he'd come to crow? 'Don't flatter yourself, Jack,' she said, briskly. 'I used to do things like that all the time. Ask my father,' she said. 'He could keep you amused for hours. I once poured glue inside the piano when I didn't practise for a concert and he wouldn't let me go to a party.' She firmly ignored the tug of anger that Jack had been able to reduce her to such behaviour. Firmly ignored the longing to reach out and touch the swelling, somehow make it better, although that was harder. Much harder. 'I thought I had grown out of such stupid temper tantrums.'

'You should never grow out of showing full-blooded emotion, Rosie.' He touched his face gingerly. 'There are, however, far more interesting ways of showing it. But if you're going to run back to Anthony you'll never find that out. He'll turn you into a dull middle-aged woman before you're thirty.'

'And you were ready to rescue me from that?' she asked, hazel eyes sparking, dangerously.

'You have a heart too big to settle for second-best, Rosie. You're the type to throw your hat over the windmill, give everything for one night that you would never forget.' He picked up her hand and raised it to his bruised cheek. 'The woman who did this last night was capable of passion on that scale. I liked her a whole lot more than the future Mrs Harlowe.'

She tried to pull away, but he

tightened his grip, forcing her to acknowledge the consequences of her passionate outburst. She met the challenge in his eyes. He didn't understand. Would never understand the sense of betrayal that had driven her to such anger. 'Well, thank you for that vote of confidence, but she won't be troubling you again.'

'I'm sorry to hear that.' He turned quickly and kissed the palm of her hand. She jerked free as if stung.

'Jack, don't . . .'

'You're really prepared to settle for a man you don't love in return for a soft billet?' His eyes were unsparing now, his voice edged with steel and she looked away, refusing to answer him, to admit that he had been right. 'Soft beds are bad for the spine, Rosie. In the long run they do far more damage than sleeping on a hard floor.'

'And is that what you are offering, Jack? A one-night stand on a hard floor? Surely a man of your apparently vast means could at least run to a bed?' She threw the barbed challenge at him.

He shook his head. 'I had to know if you really wanted me, or just someone with a bigger wallet than Anthony Harlowe.'

'Well, now you know.'

'Yes, I suppose I do. What nasty little jinx brought you to the Napier last night, Rosie? When I talked to Sarah on Monday, she told me you were staying with your mother until the weekend.' He glared at her as if she was somehow at fault. 'I hoped you would come to the party. It was to introduce everyone to Rich and I wanted to surprise you both. Well I certainly achieved the reunion. And I think most of the guests would vote it the most entertaining thrash of the year, even without the guest of honour. They particularly enjoyed the floor show.'

'I changed my plans,' she said, ignoring his jibe, slipping in one of her own. 'I was at the Napier to meet Anthony.'

'Anthony?' She had shocked him and

was glad of it. 'So where was he when you were intent on murder?'

'I never meant to hurt you, Jack.'

'No? Just plaster me with that disgusting goop. God help me if I ever do something to make you really angry.'

She exploded. 'You did make me really angry, Jack. You demanded that I turn my life upside-down for you. You're still doing it. And what are you offering in return?' She held her finger and thumb half an inch apart. 'That much. No, thank you.'

'Aren't you forgetting a long weekend when I never left your side?' he said, very quietly.

Her temper subsided as quickly as it had erupted. 'I haven't forgotten. I shall never forget. You were . . . kind.'

'Kind?' He glared at her. 'I've been called a lot of things in my life, by a lot of women. *Kind* never figured very prominently!'

'I meant it . . . ' She faltered under a scowl intensified by his battered face.

'Kindly?' he offered, with biting

sarcasm. 'We'll have to see if we can improve on the quality of your adjectives. Don't think for one moment that I've given up on you, Rosalind Parry.'

'Then you should,' she snapped back. 'I bumped into your singer at the Napier, Jack. She was most enthusiastic about you. Perhaps you should redirect your efforts in a more receptive direction.'

'The favour was offered, Rosie, and declined with thanks. She's a talented singer and worth a contract without any form of ritual sacrifice.'

'How very . . . ' She was going to say kind again, but the warning look was unmistakable ' . . . noble.'

'Good God, it gets worse. I'm not noble and right now I feel very far from kind. I simply prefer not to complicate business arrangements with meaning-less sex.'

'Well, in case you hadn't noticed, this is my place of business. Unless you have some commission that comes under that heading, I think you'd better leave right now.'

'In your case, Rosie, I could be persuaded to make an exception.' He didn't wait for a response. 'Tell me, when is the wedding? Did you say some time in May?'

She hesitated, almost too long she realised as his eyes narrowed slightly. 'A week on Tuesday,' she said, quickly. 'There didn't seem to be any point in waiting.' Not a lie, she told herself. Every word the truth.

'It's been moved forward?' he asked, rising to his feet, startled out of his easy assurance.

'There didn't seem any point in waiting,' she parroted Julie, dully.

A muscle began to work at the corner of his mouth. 'Then you don't have much time left to indulge in a little fun before you settle down with that overstuffed bore. Since you have no intention of altering your plans, presumably that was what you had in mind when you threw yourself at me in your mother's drawing room?'

Her face flamed. 'That's despicable, Jack.'

'Is it?' His eyes scalded her. 'You can't have it both ways, you know. You're going to have to make a decision and you don't have much time.' He reached for her. 'Shall I remind you what you're giving up?'

She leapt to her feet, backing away from him. 'Just go away, Jack. Go away and leave me alone.'

'Not a hope, sweetheart,' he said, his voice grating against her nerves. 'No reason to change the agenda just because our wires got scrambled. What do you say?'

She swung her hand, but he caught it and jerked her close. 'The message came through loud and clear the first time, Rosie. Don't labour the point.'

'Then why aren't you listening?' she demanded, too close to tears.

'I am listening, Rosie. You should try it yourself some time.' She tried to wrench her wrist free, but he resisted her efforts without difficulty and turned to the photograph on the wall. 'But we'll do it your way if you insist. If it's business you want, put the Lodge back on the market,' he said. 'All viewing must be accompanied by the agent. And you, Miss Parry, will do the accompanying.'

'Go to hell!'

He tutted. 'Such language. What would that nice Mr Harlowe say? Shall we ask him?' Their eyes locked, sparked, finally she lowered her lashes, giving way before his insistent gaze.

'What price are you asking?' She was trying desperately to block out the scent of his skin, the hard line of his mouth at the level of her eyes.

'I'm open to offers, Rosie,' he said, his lips twisting insolently. 'In fact, when it comes right down to it, I'm prepared to take anything I can get.' His mouth brushed hers and for a moment she swayed, shivered against him. Then she managed to wrench herself free.

'Get out! Now!'

'This is no way to treat a client, Rosie. I might have to complain to . . . '

'He'd understand,' she said, her voice barely above a whisper.

'Would he? That the woman he's about to marry comes apart at the seams whenever I touch her? Are you sure? Perhaps I should do the poor sap a favour and tell him myself.'

'Don't you dare!'

'I warned you once, Rosie, that I would dare anything for something I wanted.' His fingers traced the curve of her jaw, sending a tremor through her. 'Doesn't it occur to you that you're not being very fair to the man?'

'What do you know about being fair? Anthony . . . understands.'

'Does he?' His mouth twisted a little. 'Well, that's very convenient for you. Frankly, I don't.' He nodded, briefly and turned to go. 'I'll expect you out at the house this afternoon. Four o'clock will suit me just fine.'

'That won't be necessary.' Her voice

stayed him. 'We already have the details on our computer.'

'I'm the client. I'll decide what's necessary.'

'Very well, if you insist, but I'll have to send someone else. I already have an appointment at four,' she said, with considerable relief.

'Have you?' He glanced down at her open diary and read the name and telephone number pencilled in for her four o'clock appointment. He picked up the phone and punched in the number.

'Jack!' she protested.

He ignored her, holding her back when she would have intervened, and was forced to listen in impotent rage as he rearranged her schedule. He replaced the receiver. 'Three o'clock suits the lady just as well. Shall I make the alteration in your diary, or will you?'

'How dare you interfere?' she whispered.

'I warned you, Rosie,' he reminded her, simply. 'I'll expect you at four. Don't be late.'

Julie glanced at his retreating figure as she brought Rose a cup of tea. 'Wasn't that the man who played — '

' — the saxophone. Yes,' she agreed, quickly. 'It appears he wasn't quite what he seemed.' He'd warned her about that, but she hadn't taken any notice. 'Wickham Lodge is back on the market,' she said, firmly changing the subject.

'Oh? Well, there was another couple interested,' Julie said. 'But Mr Drayton moved so quickly and he didn't need a loan . . . was that him?' she asked, as the light suddenly dawned.

'Yes,' Rose said, without amplification. 'Maybe the other people will still be interested. Give me the file and I'll ring them now.' If they were, she might never have to go out to the Lodge and face Jack Drayton again. She pulled a face. It couldn't possibly be that easy.

'They wouldn't go to the price he paid,' Julie warned her.

'I have the feeling he's not over-bothered about the price. He's open to offers . . . ' Anything he could get — except he hadn't been talking about the house. They had both known that. She sank back into her chair. 'But I'm afraid people will think there's something wrong with the house as it's back on the market so soon.'

'I did hear something about a leaking shower. But surely that wouldn't . . . '

'Julie!' The woman's enthusiasm was suddenly too much to bear. 'You're getting married in just over a week. Haven't you got something better to do than worry about other people's houses?'

'It's all under control,' she replied, amiable in spite of Rose's irritation. 'I'm dress-hunting with my sister at the weekend and Mrs Harlowe is taking the girls out this afternoon to buy them new outfits. I've arranged to have my hair done. Is there anything else?'

'Honeymoon?' she suggested, weakly.

'We're going to Scotland.'

Rose raised her eyebrows. 'Scotland? In March?'

Julie's eyes danced with mischief. 'Does it matter?'

For a moment she thought of Jack with his hard floor and a sudden wave of longing shook her. 'No, Julie. I don't suppose it does.'

★ ★ ★

He was waiting for her when she arrived with her notebook and tape measure at precisely four o'clock. She hadn't known quite what to expect. Flirtatious perhaps, but she had been prepared for that, layering on the emotional armour as she had driven out to Wickham, reminding herself of every stupid remark, every stupid action he had led her into. Of every hurtful thing he had said about her motives for marrying Anthony.

Then he opened the door and none of it mattered. If he had put out a hand, offered half a smile she would have forgiven him. Instead he was barely polite. 'I'm glad you're on time. Shall we start upstairs?' he began, without preamble.

'Whatever you say . . . ' She caught herself, half expecting the usual teasing remark in response. There was nothing, just a cool stare. To her intense chagrin she found herself colouring. She turned abruptly away and led the way up the stairs, opening the first door she came to. His bedroom. She self-consciously cleared her throat. 'Master bedroom with en suite bathroom,' she read from her details. 'Do you want to check the room sizes?'

'I want to check everything,' he said. 'Would you like me to help?'

'You'll have to,' she replied. She would normally have brought a junior to assist her on this kind of job, but clearly they would have thought her quite mad. 'Will you take the tape, please.' They solemnly remeasured the room and she noted the dimensions on her pad. 'The same as last time.' She was unable to resist adding, 'Amazing.' Rose wound in the tape. He didn't let go and she physically jumped as her fingers brushed his. She looked up uncertainly, but his expression was unreadable.

'Why don't we stop this right now, Rosie?' he asked intently. 'Right here.' He turned her to face the bed. 'It's what we both want.'

'Are you including all the furniture and fittings?' she asked, clinging to the notepad to stop her hands from shaking, hoping that her voice was steadier than her heartbeat.

'Furniture is no good without a house to put it in,' he responded, as if the conversation were perfectly normal.

She made a note, took a breath. Kept her eyes firmly fixed on the pad. 'Do you agree with the description of the bathroom?' she asked. 'Or do we have to go through this item by item?' He made no answer and she was forced to look up to find him regarding her intently. 'Well?'

'Item by item, I think.' He very gently touched her lips with the tips of his fingers. " . . . as, item, two lips, indifferent red; item, two grey eyes with lids to them . . . "

'My eyes aren't grey.'

He ignored her protest, stroked her neck with the back of his fingers and smiled as he felt her quiver beneath his touch. ' ' . . . item, one neck, one chin . . . ' ' He tilted it upwards. If he kissed her every semblance of control would evaporate. She stepped back quickly and he made no attempt to hold her.

'This will take hours,' she warned.

'I'm in no hurry, Rosie,' he said, softly. He turned and opened the bathroom door. For a moment she hesitated, then stepped inside and Jack leaned against the door, watching her as she checked off the fittings against her list.

'Everything is there,' she said. 'Shall we get on?'

'I would like your opinion about this shower. You've used it,' he reminded her. 'Do you think it's big enough for two? It could be an interesting selling point.'

'I can't put that down!'

'You can if I insist. But I think we'd better make sure.' He took the pad from her and put it down. 'After you.'

'Don't be ridiculous, Jack,' she warned.

He didn't bother to argue, but put his hands around her waist and lifted her from her feet. 'Shoes off, I think.' He shook her slightly and they fell to the floor with a clunk. Then he stepped with her into the shower stall and lowered her to the floor, keeping his hands fastened around her waist. 'There seems plenty of room to me. What do you think? Why don't you see if you can reach the soap?'

Being held by him, inches from his chest, was an exquisite kind of torture. Every instinct was urging her to throw caution to the wind, take what he was offering, no matter how little. But Rosalind was beginning to understand what he meant by total commitment.

She didn't just want his body. It had to be everything or nothing. She reached for the soap, wanting to get this farce over with as quickly as possible, but as she raised her arm, he drew her hard into his body.

'On second thoughts, I believe we should try it properly.' His voice grated against every nerve-ending and a short, fierce breath escaped her lips as her hard-won control began to crumble at this assault on her senses.

He reached for the tap and a cascade of warm water engulfed them. He captured her face in his hands and began unhurriedly to kiss her as the water streamed down her face. There was a kind of primeval glory about it and she wanted to be out of her clothes and in his arms. Then he raised his head and she saw from the gleam of barely disguised triumph in his eyes that he knew he had won. As he began to unfasten the buttons of her blouse she reached mindlessly for the tap and flipped it over to cold.

9

For a scant second nothing happened. Then, as a fierce stream of cold water caught the back of his neck he abruptly released her and she stepped clear.

'Definitely large enough for two. But I think the rest of the details are accurate enough,' she said, ignoring the fact that she was soaking wet and water was dripping over her notes and the ink was running all over the place. He turned off the water and stepped from the shower, stripping off his T-shirt in one smooth movement and discarding it. His hands were already at the fastening of his trousers and she stood rooted to the spot.

'What are you doing?' she gasped.

'I'm taking my clothes off, Rosie. And when I've done that, I'm going to take off yours.'

She didn't wait to see if he meant it

but turned and fled, barefoot and dripping, to the safety of her car.

* ★ *

If Rosalind had hoped that interest in the house would be minimal she was to be disappointed. Every day she had to drive out to Wickham two or three times to show prospective purchasers over the property. Endure the contempt in his eyes. The first time he had solemnly handed her the pair of shoes she had abandoned in her flight. 'Miss Parry left in a bit of a hurry last time,' he offered in explanation to the woman who had come to view the Lodge, and Rose had had to suffer that lady's barely contained curiosity as they had toured the house.

'How many days is it now to the wedding, Rosie?' he asked each time he saw her and she answered without comment. 'Looking forward to it?' he asked once, trying to provoke some response. 'You look a bit pale, but perhaps that's just bridal nerves? I'd be nervous if I was marrying Anthony.'

'Anthony wouldn't be very happy about it, either.'

To punish her he chose to follow them around the house, chatting easily to the middle-aged couple who seemed very keen. 'The house is being sold as it is,' he reminded them. 'With all the furniture.' They were in the master bedroom and he leaned against the doorway. 'Why don't you tell them how comfortable the bed is, Rosie?' She stiffened, but they took no notice, apparently absorbed in size of the fitted cupboards.

Since the incident with the shower she had been very careful not to be alone with him. All business contact had been via Julie and at home she had stopped answering the telephone, but if he phoned her there she didn't know. He didn't leave any messages on her answering machine.

Every time she went to the car park for her car she half expected him to appear. Every time the office door clanged she jumped. After a week which almost reduced her to a nervous wreck she was at last beginning to relax, believing he had finally got the point.

Then a couple with a small boy made an appointment to view the Lodge. The child was clearly bored to death with house-hunting and Jack took pity on him and led him away to play games on his computer down in the study.

After the parents had seen everything, the child was still stretched out on the floor alongside Jack, several layers down in a dungeon, fighting his way out with a little help. 'Throw in the computer and the game and I'll make an offer for the house now,' the child's father joked.

Jack turned from the screen, briefly. 'Sorry. The computer's no problem, but the game is a prototype. It's still under development.'

'Is that what you do? Develop games software?'

'Mr Drayton loves to play games,'

Rose said, without any thought of the consequences. 'It's what he does best.' It was the first time she had let the professional veneer slip. Jack rolled on to his side and stared up at her.

'I sense disapproval. More over lad, we'll have to teach the lady to show a little respect.'

The boy wriggled over without taking his eyes from the screen. 'Very funny, Jack,' she said, backing away. 'But I'm afraid I have another appointment — '

'Here, in about twenty minutes. You might just as well stay.' It was true. She had planned to drive a little way down the road to a layby and wait there. He patted the floor beside him. 'Come along, Rosie. No need to be shy,' he said. 'I'll show you what to do.'

The couple exchanged a glance and retrieved their son. 'We'll see ourselves out.'

'Well, Rosie? What's the matter? It's only a game, after all. You've the rest of your life for the serious stuff.' She didn't think he was talking about the game on screen, but she was unable to move, unable to advance or retreat. He rolled on to his back and lay propped on his elbows while mayhem erupted upon the screen behind him.

'I think you've lost, Jack,' she said, hoarsely, as 'Game Over' flashed up on the screen.

'Don't be too sure, Rosie.' He rose in one smooth movement and she was trapped on the wrong side of the door. 'It's never over until the fat lady sings.' She jumped as he took her hand. He smiled, apparently satisfied at this evidence that he still had the power to evoke an instant response from her. 'Come along, I'll show you.' He led her back to the computer. 'While we're waiting?'

'Waiting?'

'For the next group of tourists to troop through the stately home.'

'Jack, why are you doing this to me? You've had your fun.'

'And paid for it.' He ran a finger over the still vivid bruising of his cheek but she refused to be drawn into another apology. 'Humour me. What have you got to worry about, after all? You're getting married tomorrow. Nearly safe home.'

'This is silly,' she said, gesturing at the screen.

'I know. Everyone thinks it's silly. My accountant thinks it's hysterical.'

'Oh, very well,' she said, glancing at her watch. It was already well past five o'clock and her next appointment was in just over a quarter of an hour. If she left it would be tantamount to admitting that she was afraid to stay. At least playing his stupid game she wouldn't have to indulge in verbal gymnastics simply to keep one step ahead of him. 'But you'd better hope that one of today's applicants buys this place, because this is the very last time I'm coming out here.'

She knelt down in front of the VDU and he handed her a control paddle. 'With the wedding tomorrow, Rosie, that hardly comes as a great surprise.

What does surprise me is that you're working at all. Can't you bear to be away from Anthony for more than half an hour at a time?'

She knew she should own up. 'Jack . . . '

'Yes?'

She couldn't do it. Not now. Not here. She was too vulnerable. If she told him, he would know that he had won and she would be at his mercy. She glanced at her watch again. Fifteen minutes. She hoped Mr Fulton wouldn't be late. 'Nothing. How's the club coming along,' she asked, desperate for some neutral subject.

'I've no idea. I haven't been near the place. You'd better ask your father. It's his baby now.' He restarted the game. 'Or did you think I'd throw a tantrum and sack him after your little display of temper put me in Casualty?'

'No.' She held up the paddle. 'What am I supposed to be doing with this?'

'Thank you for that, anyway. Here, it's easier if you stretch out.' She kicked off her shoes and lay flat on her stomach. 'Now, take it like this.' He settled beside her, draped his arm around her shoulders, as he helped her to direct it. She was about to protest, but instead jumped as a fearsome monster disappeared to the realistic sound of a death rattle and he tightened his grip. She tried to shift away. 'Watch the screen,' he commanded. 'Total concentration. Was your mother glad to see him?'

'I don't know. I haven't been home. I thought it was better to leave them alone for a while to sort out their problems.'

'Well, it'll be nice to have him around tomorrow to give you away.'

'Give me . . . ' Ashamed, she turned away to hide the heat that seared across her cheekbones. 'Yes.'

'Concentrate, Rosie, or you'll get eaten. Look out!' A giant spider dropped from above with a blood-curdling screech and she screamed and dropped the paddle, turning away from the screen and burying her face in the soft wool of his shirt. 'Realistic, isn't it?' he said, gravely, holding her lightly.

'Why do people play this?' she asked, a little breathlessly. He caught her chin in his hand and tilted it gently upwards.

'They enjoy the excitement, the risk. Don't you feel it?'

'No,' she said, quickly and returned her attention to the safer dangers on the screen. He handed her back the paddle.

'Try again, Rosie. You'll soon get the hang of it. Tell me,' he said, glancing sideways at her, his arm once more about her shoulder, his hand firmly directing hers. But now there was no sense of the game. It was just a background noise to the sensations that were pouring through her. Bewildering, disconcerting. 'Where did you finally settle on for the honeymoon? Is it going to be culture, or ruins?'

'Ruins?' She asked vaguely. She had no idea what he was talking about. She was only aware of the warmth of his arm around her shoulder, the touch of his fingers on hers.

'That was the plan, wasn't it?' He rolled away from her and she almost cried out at this desertion. He lay on his side propped up on his elbow, watching her as she tried helplessly to escape a horde of killer bees without his help. He reached over and removed a pin from her hair. 'Is it still lots of sightseeing in Italy?'

'Italy?' She gasped as he drew her close against him, moulding her body to his and helped himself to another pin. On the screen, a dozen aliens died unnoticed.

She dropped the paddle, put up her hands to prevent his raiding fingers. 'Jack, don't,' she murmured, but there was no conviction in her voice. Because she didn't want him to stop.

'You should always wear your hair loose, Rosie.' Another pin and the chignon began to slide and nothing would save it now. He ran his fingers through it, shaking it loose and his touch on her scalp was like a drug, instantly addictive and when he took his hand away she moaned softly.

All the days she had been coming to the house, fending off the teasing, holding herself aloof, had built up the tension within her. Now, at his touch it was as if the dam had suddenly been breached and nothing could stop the flood of passion from spilling over and submerging them both.

'Run now, Rosie,' he murmured, and the sound of his voice stroked over her skin like velvet. 'If you can.' But she was unable to move. Boneless, weak, as if she had been driven at high speed. Her breathing was shallow, her lids were half-closed, her lips parted waiting for him. He took a handful of her hair in his long fingers and in one swift movement bound her to him.

His lips fluttered briefly against her eyelids, touched the finely modelled cheekbones, followed the curve of her jaw to the tip of her chin. She sighed and reached up for him, letting her hands explore his face. He remained quite still while the pads of her fingers moved gently over the bruised cheek, the raw scar. She stroked his temples, traced the strong brows, outlined the fierce, proud mouth. Her hands needed no schooling. They moved instinctively over his neck and throat until they reached the barrier of his shirt. Then they began to undo the buttons.

Her eyes remembered the broad chest, the dark sprinkling of hair that was rough under her fingers. He seized her hands, preventing her further exploration. A small complaint escaped her lips. 'You're mine now, Rose.' His voice was husky, his eyes dark above her. 'There's no escape.'

His tongue outlined her full, ripe mouth and she reached for him greedily, dragging him down to explore the exciting depths of his mouth and make them her own, the world forgotten in her impatience as she arched against him, proud to feel the urgent response of his body against hers. He groaned. 'Witch. You've got to be a witch.'

* * *

When she woke, the sun was streaming in through the window. She felt like a child on Christmas morning. Exultant, brand new. For a brief, confused moment she wasn't sure why, then Jack shifted beside her, throwing his arm about her in his sleep and the joy of it all came flooding back. She turned on her side to look at him. Treasuring the way his face crumpled against his pillow, the strength of square tanned shoulders and a well muscled back. A lock of hair had fallen over his forehead giving him an oddly boyish look and he was smiling in his sleep.

She lay for a while contemplating the pleasures of a night that on reflection had involved not one, but a considerable quantity of caps being tossed over windmills. The thick carpet of the study floor had absorbed the impact of that first explosive union when neither of them could wait another second. Afterwards he had simply picked her up and carried her up to his bed.

Sometime in the night he had raided the kitchen and come back to bed with a tray of food. It was only then she remembered Mr Fulton. The reason she had been able to relax, felt so safe was that any moment he would ring the doorbell wanting to view Wickham Lodge and rescue her. But Mr Fulton had never arrived.

'There was no appointment,' Jack said, when Rose mentioned it.

Rosalind frowned. 'But I spoke to the man myself. I'd never heard of him, so I phoned his office to check he was genuine.'

'Oh, Mr Fulton is real enough,' Jack agreed, with a grin. 'He works for me.'

'He . . . I think you'd better explain, Mr Drayton,' she said, severely.

'Do I have to? Think about it, Rosie. How else was I going to keep you here, all to myself for a while? I was beginning to run out of ideas.'

'You underestimate yourself.'

'No. I underestimated you. I thought while I kept you coming to the house you might just realise how much I wanted you, Rose. How much you wanted me. And you kept coming. Detached, cool, professional, this beautiful hair pinned to perfection. Lord, if you knew what those horrible hairpins did to me. I wanted to rip them out, carry you up here and make wild and passionate love to you.'

'You were going to miss out the study floor?' she enquired, affecting surprise.

'That was your fault, my darling. You were . . . how can I put it? Impatient?'

'I wasn't complaining.' She pulled a face. 'You can correct me if my memory is at fault, Jack Drayton, but you seemed quite enthusiastic yourself!'

His mouth curved in a lazy smile. 'Guilty, ma'am, as charged.' He leaned across and kissed her shoulder. 'In fact, it's quite incredible how enthusiastic I am.'

'Jack . . . I must tell you . . . ' His lips touched hers and she caught her breath as once more the fire surged through her veins.

'Later, sweetheart,' he murmured, as he bore her back down to the bed. And she let it go. Somehow the moment didn't seem quite right to break the news that she wasn't about to be married. He might think she expected him to step into Anthony's place and she didn't want that. Besides, it didn't matter. He'd know soon enough. Then he began to make love to her so tenderly that she forgot about everything except the joy of lying in the arms of the man she loved, knowing that he wanted her.

* * *

Rosalind Parry looked down at the figure lying alongside her, her eyes feasting on the smooth tanned skin of his back, the way his hair curled darkly on to his neck. He breathed the slow,

266

even tempo of a man deep in sleep and she smiled and was finally unable to resist the temptation to kiss his shoulder.

She moved carefully, wanting to take him by surprise, wake him gradually with her lips, but as she bent to this delightful task she caught sight of the clock at the side of the bed. It was late. Nearly ten o'clock. Not that it mattered, because she wasn't going to work today. She frowned at the thought. That was wrong surely? It was Tuesday. Then she remembered why she wasn't going to work.

Regretfully she drew back. No reason to wake him now. There wasn't even time for an explanation. She would leave a note. When she came back would be time enough to tell him everything. Right now, she should be wearing her best suit and heading for the register office. Heaven knew that she didn't want to go. But she had promised and in some way she couldn't quite understand, it was a last act, drawing a line under her relationship with Anthony.

She eased herself out of the big bed. He stirred, rolled over onto his back and she held her breath until the even breathing resumed. Then she opened the door and tiptoed down the stairs.

Her clothes were still scattered across the study, an eloquent testament to the urgency of their passion. She scrambled into them without worrying too much about the niceties of buttons then looked for a pad, something to write on. The desk was a monument to modern technology. But bereft of anything as simple as a pencil and notepad. Rose glanced at her watch. There was no more time. Besides, what need was there for a note? She had shown him all her deepest feelings last night and she would be back almost before he had had time to miss her.

She closed the door quietly behind her and climbed into her car although she felt as if she could have flown all the way home, without the benefit of wheels or an engine, on the high of joyful euphoria.

Her shower was brief, her make-up sketchy and even if she had the time to do her hair in its customary chignon, her hairpins were strewn across Jack's study floor. So she jammed it up under her hat and hoped it would stay there. After all, no one would be looking at her today.

But she was shaking so much when she arrived at the register office that she almost fell into the seat next to Julie's children. Julie and Anthony took their places in front of the registrar and the ceremony began.

The registrar's voice droned on, explaining that marriage was a binding commitment. Julie looked so pretty, she thought absently. She was wearing a fitted cream suit and a hat that should have been too big for her, but somehow wasn't. She couldn't see her face, but she could picture it. Wonderfully calm. She never seemed to get flustered, or lose her temper. She would make

Anthony a wonderful wife. And despite her regret at having to leave Jack asleep in his big bed, she was glad she had come. The ceremony moved on. The couple made their promises.

She heard the door open behind them. The registrar looked up and frowned at the interruption from a late arrival. One of Julie's daughters asked in a loud whisper how much longer it would take and she bent quickly to reassure her that it was nearly over. The registrar declared the couple man and wife and Anthony turned to Julie. He looked almost shell-shocked with happiness as he kissed her. The door at the back clicked shut. She turned then, but whoever it was had gone. Wrong wedding, she supposed. Too late, or too early.

It was more than an hour before she was able to escape the buffet lunch that Mrs Harlowe had arranged for the couple. She couldn't be the first to leave. It would be noticed, remarked on. She stuck it out, hardly aware of what she was eating, or remarks addressed to her, her head still floating in her own cloud of happiness.

Finally, people began to move and she was at last released from duty.

Her first thought was to go straight back. She had a picture of Jack still in bed, waiting for her. Then reality suggested that was ridiculous and that arriving in her wedding outfit, complete with pink rosebud, was a bit over the top. She went back to her flat. Showered, washed her hair. Changed into a pair of jeans and a shirt. Then she drove back to Wickham.

She pulled up in the courtyard. The sun was shining on the mellow stone, reflecting off the windows. Daffodils in tubs shone back.

She approached the front door, half expecting it to be thrown open, scooped up into his arms. It remained shut. He obviously hadn't heard the car. Should she ring the bell? Go round to the back to the kitchen door? Or she had a bunch of keys. She could let herself in.

The protocol of such a situation was beyond her. In the end she rang the bell but there was no reply.

She stood on the doorstep feeling a little foolish. Then she shrugged. She was being stupid. He was probably in the shower, or absorbed in one of his games. She took out the keys with the Nightingale and Drake tag and let herself in.

'Jack?' she called. 'I'm back.' There was no answer. The house was silent. She took a step inside and shut the door. 'Jack?' she called again.

She glanced in the study, went through to the kitchen. There was no sign of him. In a sudden fit of panic she ran up the stairs, certain that something had happened to him. She threw open the bedroom door and stopped on the threshold, unable to believe her eyes.

The room was empty. The bed had been stripped. All trace of Jack had gone. The wardrobe doors stood untidily open, their interiors bare. She slowly crossed the room and closed them.

His things had gone from the bathroom. The shelves were bare. He had gone.

It took a while to sink in. He'd had his one-night stand and, if the floor hadn't been particularly hard, he had proved his point. And he hadn't even had to tell her. No scene. She had left his bed high as a kite on happiness and he had taken the opportunity to leave. How long had he waited? she wondered. Not long. She had been away just a little more than four hours.

The wave of nausea hit her like an express train and it seemed forever before she stopped being sick. She sat on the bathroom floor with her cheek pressed against the cold marble panelling for a long time before she found sufficient strength to stand. She didn't bother to rush. It didn't matter how long she took. One thing was certain. Jack Drayton was not coming back to intrude on her agony.

Her legs were weak as she finally made it down the stairs and she leaned for a moment against the study doorway. She saw the desk. Had he left a note? Some word of explanation? Her heart in her mouth she walked the few feet. But there was no note.

She went round the house, automatically doing what she did best, her job. She checked the windows and doors. Made certain everything was secure. Finally the key turned in the front door, locking away her happiness, her dreams. She blinked back a tear. She would carry on. Go through the motions of living. She would have to. But she wasn't quite sure how.

She climbed into her car and started the engine. One step at a time. One day at a time. It wouldn't be the sort of life she had planned. But she had a career, a job that she loved. It would be a start. Maybe it would have to be enough.

★　★　★

When Sarah came home from work she found Rosalind sitting in the dark.

'Good lord,' she said, as she switched on the light and found her there. 'You gave me a fright. What on earth are you doing?'

'I think I must have dozed off,' she lied.

'Late night, was it? I didn't hear you come in.'

'I didn't come in. I stayed the night at Wickham Lodge with Jack.'

Sarah gave a little shrug. 'Well, I wouldn't have said anything, but I did sort of notice you weren't here.' She bustled through to the kitchen. 'Do want a cup of something?' There was no answer and she came back and looked at Rose and gave a little sigh. 'Do you want to talk about it?'

'Talk about it?' she asked, dully. 'What do you want, Sarah? All the sordid details?'

Sarah sat on the arm of the chair and put her arms around her. 'The details will keep, love. But I think you'd better let some of it out. It might help.'

'Nothing will help.' Rose made an

awkward, dismissive little gesture. 'It was a lovely wedding . . . ' Her voice broke on a sob. 'Oh, Sarah. How on earth could I have been so stupid. I walked right into it. I only had to say no. He would have let me go and I would have been free.'

'I don't expect you wanted to be free, Rose. That's the way it is. No sense in it. I didn't think he'd hurt you, though. I thought . . . ' She shook her head. 'I thought he was in love with you.'

Rose stared at her blankly. 'No. He never said that. He said he wanted me. That's not quite the same, is it?'

'You can never tell with men. They don't use the same words that we do. Do you want to tell me what happened?'

'Nothing happened.' She shook her head. 'No, that's not right. Quite a lot happened. Then I had to go to the wedding because I'd promised Julie. He was asleep. I didn't wake him, because there didn't seem to be any reason. When I went back he had gone.

Everything. Not even a note.'

Sarah drew in a sharp breath. 'Bastard!'

'Possibly,' Rose said, very carefully.

'Oh, God. You never used anything?'

She gave an odd little laugh. 'No, Sarah. Rather careless of me. With Anthony, the situation never seemed to arise. With Jack . . . ' Jack had obliterated everything but the moment.

'What'll you do?'

'Wait. That's what women do, isn't it? I love him, Sarah. If it's to be, then I'll love his child.' With the words spoken, the reality faced, she felt stronger. 'Then it won't have been a complete waste. Come on. Let's get something to eat.'

'Rose?'

'I'm hungry, Sarah.'

The next day she received an offer for Wickham Lodge. She explained quite calmly that the owner wasn't available at the moment, but she would write and put it to him. That was all she could do. Perhaps he had arranged for his mail to be forwarded. It was a standard letter from the partners, formal, brief. She had a late appointment and left her senior negotiator to sign the mail. Writing her name on a letter to him would have seemed like begging.

After two weeks, the prospective buyer was getting anxious and she was left with no choice but to telephone her father at the club. He was delighted to hear from her.

'When are you coming to see us then, *cariad?*' he asked.

'Us? You're home? With Mother?'

'I tiptoed in at the french windows and she was in my arms before she had time to think about it. You're a clever girl.'

'Don't break her heart again, Dada,' she warned.

'No, Rosie. I'm home for good. We're going to sell the house and move into Melchester. I suppose you'd better take care of the details for us. Come down at the weekend and measure everything up.'

'Mum's giving up her job?' she asked, in surprise.

'She's been offered a post in the Local Education Authority. She wasn't going to take it, but it fits in very well with my job at the club.'

The reference to the club brought her back to the point of the call. 'Dada, can you tell me where Jack Drayton is? We've had an offer for his house, but he isn't replying to his mail.'

'He'd have a job to do that, *cariad*. He's in the United States.'

So far away. At least there was no danger of walking into him. Of him turning up in the office. 'Have you got an address? Or a telephone number?'

'No. He's moving about a lot. But if he phones I'll tell him you rang.'

'Just tell him Nightingale and Drake, Dada. It isn't personal.'

Her father laughed, softly. 'Got him out of your system with that tin tray, did you, my Rosie?'

No. Not out of her system. He was locked in there, growing, developing, a part of her. She hadn't even told Sarah, yet. It was too soon to be certain. But she knew. Had no doubt. It would be just her secret for a little while, before she had to let the world in. 'Goodbye, Dada. I'll see you soon.'

Her heart jumped every time the phone rang for a week until she was a nervous wreck. But Jack didn't phone and when she asked Mr Nightingale for advice on the situation he rather tetchily told her to take the house off the market.

She filed it away under 'pending'. Appropriate, she thought, rather like her life. Waiting.

10

Sarah could not be fooled for long. The first time Rose was sick, she pounced.

'What are you going to do?' she demanded.

'Nothing.'

'You have to tell him. He has a right to know.'

'Has he? I don't think so. For him it was all a game. A bit of fun. He kissed me and I lit up like a Christmas tree.' She found herself smiling at the memory. 'I imagine most women would. And most of them would have fallen straight into his bed. It took me a while to get around to it, but he made it in the end. Game over.'

'I can't believe it was like that,' Sarah protested. 'The way he looked after you when you were sick ... most men would have run a mile.'

'Yes, but Jack isn't most men, he likes

to play games.' It had taken her a while to fathom it out, but she'd had a lot of time for thinking in the last couple of weeks. 'It's what he's good at, Sarah. Very good. I'm not surprised it's made him a lot of money.' Sarah looked doubtful. 'Think about it. Most men would have used their wealth to dazzle a girl. He could even have used the fact that he had met my father as a way to interest me. But I gave him another lever. Showed him the way in. I thought he was down on his luck and tried to help him. And he let me do just that.'

'He had a funny way of repaying you.'

'Well, I suppose it all got a bit out of hand when I found out that he wasn't quite what he had allowed me to believe.' She told Sarah about meeting the singer from the jazz club and the incident with the salmon mousse.

'And I thought you lived a dull life. You've certainly been having a busy time while I've been staying with Matt.'

She chuckled. 'Lord, I wish I'd been there to see it. Three stitches, you said?'

'I'm not proud of it, Sarah. I could have caused him a serious injury.'

'Well, he certainly got his own back. His face will heal, with just a faint scar to add a little mystery, a little extra attraction. But one way or another your life has been changed permanently. The least he can do is give you some support. If he's as wealthy as you say, he won't even notice.'

'Just another standing order? Along with the credit cards and the electricity bill. No, I don't think so, Sarah. I'll manage.'

'How?'

'I'll manage,' she said, stubbornly.

'Think about it, Rose. And while you're thinking about that, give some thought about what you're going to tell your parents. Your father might not be quite so laid back about it as you appear to be. Mr Nightingale might have a few words on the subject as well.'

'I'll take maternity leave and I'll find a childminder.'

'No doubt. When you've paid for her, you might give some thought about what the two of you will live on. Or are you planning to move back in with your parents?'

'No! Don't be so negative, Sarah. Lots of people do it. Julie brought up two children on her own.'

'I'm not saying you can't do it, love, just that it doesn't have to be quite that hard. Let him know.'

She shrugged. 'Not so easy. I've been trying to get in touch with him for weeks about the house.'

'Surely he's got an office?'

Rose gave a little gasp. 'Of course. Mr Fulton. Why on earth didn't I try him before?' She picked up her brief case and found her diary. 'I must have his number . . . yes. Too late now. I'll ring him in the morning.'

'You will tell him, then? You've finally seen sense?'

'What? Oh, about the baby. No,

Sarah. That subject is closed. I was simply thinking about the house.' She smiled a little wryly. 'After all, I'm going to need all the commission I can get, don't you think?'

* * *

Mr Fulton was wary. 'Is this a personal matter, Miss Parry?' he asked.

She wondered if he had been warned that she might try to get in touch. Whether he knew the purpose of his little deception. Her cheeks burned, but her voice was cool. 'No, Mr Fulton. I have no personal business with Mr Drayton. I'm calling on behalf of Nightingale and Drake. We've had an offer for the Lodge. We have written, but received no reply.' She finally retreated behind the senior partner. 'Mr Nightingale would like to know whether Mr Drayton wishes to proceed or whether we should withdraw the house from the market.'

The man was discouraging. 'Jack's

somewhere in the States, Miss Parry. He might be doing any one of a dozen things. I can leave messages at likely places and maybe he'll pick one of them up, but I'm not expecting him back for at least six months.'

'I see.' She was a little sharp, certain that the man knew more than he was saying. Had he been told not to give any information about his whereabouts to Rosalind Parry? 'And you can run his companies without him for all that time?'

The man paused. 'It may sound an odd sort of arrangement, but Jack's the thinking man behind this operation. It's what he does best. He's leaves the commercial side of things to people who know what they're doing.'

'But you don't feel empowered to make a decision on this particular matter?'

'Well, this isn't business, is it, Miss Parry? This is personal.' There was something contemptuous in the man's voice. Something knowing. And suddenly everything fell into place.

'Have we met, Mr Fulton?' she asked.

'We weren't formally introduced. You had other things on your mind at the time and you departed somewhat hurriedly. But the impression remains indelible.'

She was right, he had been one of the men sitting with Jack at the Napier. 'I left you rather a mess to clean up, Mr Fulton, but then I imagine you must be used to it. Tell me,' she asked, scornfully, 'do you always do Jack's dirty work for him?'

When he replied, the man's voice was touched with steel. 'I'd do anything for Jack Drayton. He's my friend as well as my boss and from the look of him when I took him to the airport, he's had about as much of you as he can take.' She tried to speak. To protest. Her mouth opened but nothing came out. But the man hadn't finished with her. 'I'll try and get an answer about the house for you, Miss Parry, if it's that important to you. Then perhaps you'll leave him alone so that he can draw a line under the experience and begin to forget all about you.' He hung up.

She continued to sit at her desk, the telephone to her ear, until the dialling tone changed to a high-pitched note. He had sounded as if he blamed her for something, almost as if he hated her. She stared at the receiver as if unaware of the reason she was holding it, then replaced it carefully on the receiver. Something dropped on to the pad in front of her and she glanced down. A second tear splashed there and puddled the ink.

★   ★   ★

Rosalind broke the news that they were about to become grandparents to her mother and father at the weekend. Her father's Celtic fire seared her ears temporarily, those of the absent father of her baby for considerably longer, and she took it without flinching. Her mother's response appeared to be mainly irritation that a woman of her age could have been so careless.

'First you let a steady man like Anthony slip through your fingers . . . then this.'

'He didn't slip, Mother. I pushed him.'

'For a musician! Don't you know they're nothing but trouble?' She glanced at her husband and her face softened. 'Oh, lord, who am I to blame you? Don't fret, my dear. We'll cope.'

'What do you want us to do, *cariad?*'

'Nothing, Dada. I just wanted you to know before you began to notice for yourselves.'

'And Mr Drayton?' her mother asked. 'What has he to say regarding approaching fatherhood?'

There had been little point in trying to hide the identity of the baby's father since they had both immediately jumped to the same, no doubt quite obvious conclusion. 'He doesn't know anything about it.'

'I do hope that he has some recollection — ' her mother began, but Rose stopped her.

'He doesn't know about the baby, Mother, and I have no intention of telling him. I don't want anyone else doing it on my behalf. I shan't be seeing him again. Ever.' She looked at her father. 'I want your promise.'

For a moment he looked as if he would challenge her. Then, catching his wife's eye, he shrugged. 'All right, Rosie. Have it your own way. We'll do everything we can for you, you know that.'

It was odd. She had hated Jack calling her Rosie because it reminded her of her absent father. Now it was her father reminding her of Jack. It took every ounce of self-control to keep herself together, but she made it, just and managed to smile as well.

'All I want from you right now is a hand with this tape measure so that I can get on with finding a buyer for this house,' she said, firmly changing the subject. 'Have you looked at anything in Melchester yet?'

'No. We were thinking of something a bit smaller. But perhaps now . . . well, we might look for something we could all share together. What do you say?'

'No, Dada. I have to live my own life. So do you.'

He turned to his wife for support. 'Rosie will do exactly as she wants,' she said. 'She always has.' She didn't add 'like her father'. She didn't have to.

Rose and her father exchanged a guilty look and crept off to measure up the rest of the house.

But despite the awkward revelation of her pregnancy it had been a happy weekend. She was quite sorry when Sunday evening came and it was time to go back to the flat.

Rich Parry carried her bag to the car. 'The club is reopening next week, Rose. We've a supper concert planned, and a lot of old friends are playing. Will you come?'

She shook her head. 'I don't think so, Dada.'

He shrugged. 'Seems a pity. It'll be fun. And I don't seriously think there's any danger of Jack turning up for it, do you?'

'Frankly, no. His office don't expect him back for six months at least.'

'You have tried to speak to him, then?'

'Only about business. And I shan't do that again.' She stopped by the car. 'I did mean what I said. I don't want him to know about the baby.' She shivered, slightly. She wasn't a fool. She knew how hard it was going to be. She'd spent the past week working out the financial situation. *In extremis* she might finally have conceded to common sense and applied to Jack for assistance. Until she had spoken to Fulton.

'I gave you my word, Rosie.'

'I know you'll keep it.'

'Then come to the club. For me. Your mother has graciously agreed to come. You would be company for her. Bring

Sarah and her boyfriend, too. Make up a party.' He gave her arm a little shake. 'Life doesn't stop, sweetheart.'

'Of course it doesn't. In fact, I'll do better than that. I'll bring everyone from the office. They all deserve a treat. It's been a long winter.'

'That's the spirit.' He grinned. 'And in the meantime look about for a house that can be divided nicely into two.'

She found everyone enthusiastic about a night at the relaunched jazz club. They arrived early, were given a guided tour by Rich and then settled in some state at a table with a good view of the small stage.

'It's lovely, Dada. Transformed,' she said, as they walked around the buffet, helping themselves to food, accompanied by the music of an enthusiastic young Dutch group.

'All it took was money, and there was no shortage of that.'

'And a lot of enthusiasm.'

'That wasn't in short supply, either. I think your mother is impressed. I thought I'd have to drag her kicking and screaming into this sink of iniquity.'

Rose laughed. 'Don't exagerrate. She looks perfectly happy. You both look happy. Are you?'

'Yes, thank you, my child. We have both of us mellowed a little with the passing years. And looking forward to the prospect of becoming grand — '

'Shhh! That's still on the classified list as far as the office is concerned.'

'Oh, right.' He glanced at her plate as she turned back to the table. 'Have you got enough to eat?'

'Plenty, thanks.'

'Not hankering for a little salmon mousse?' he asked, teasing her. 'I thought it safer to cross it off the caterer's list.'

'If I don't see another one for twenty years it will still be too soon,' she confessed. Then chuckled. 'But your lovely club is safe. I have sworn a solemn oath never to throw another plate in my life.'

They rejoined the others at their

table, drank a little wine, listened to the music. Later, when the dishes had been cleared, it was the turn of the serious musicians. The club was crowded, but when Rich Parry began to play there wasn't a sound to be heard. Rose turned to her mother, was stunned to see that proud and somewhat fierce lady sitting with tears streaming down her face. 'I didn't know,' she said. 'Heaven help me, I didn't know he was that good.' Afterwards, when the enraptured audience finally let him go, her mother excused herself and hurried backstage.

There was a moment's hiatus in the proceedings. The stage remained in darkness. People began to shift impatiently in their seats. Then there was a note. Almost undetectable. Low at first. Low, blue, heart-stoppingly intense. It grew out of the darkness, climbing steadily, rising and the audience held its collective breath. Waiting. Then the sound burst upwards, outwards, filled the room and the narrow beam of the spotlight finally fell on the black-clad figure bent over the saxophone, touching the darkness of his hair, gleaming off the instrument, only his face was left in shadow. Alone on the stage, propped casually on a tall stool, he played as if no one else in the world could hear him.

Rose wanted to run. Escape. Hide from him and the sweet, searching music. But she couldn't. She was pinned to her seat by long, haunting minor chords that evoked every feeling, every gesture of the man. It was as if he was making love to her through music. His hands played the keys as if they were her body, sure of his touch, tormenting and tender by turns. Stroking every last response from her, every final gasp of pleasure until she could stand no more and crashed headlong into oblivion.

★   ★   ★

Her eyes half opened, flickered uncertainly against the light. It was too bright and she closed them again. 'She's coming round.' It was her father's voice.

The door opened and the room fell silent. 'What happened?' His voice was hard. Almost unrecognisable.

'She fainted,' Rich Parry answered, sharply. 'She's had a shock. What the devil did you think you were playing at, turning up unannounced, helping yourself to the stage the minute my back was turned? I promised her you wouldn't be here tonight.'

'A little presumptuous of you, Rich. This is my club, after all. It was always my intention to play on the opening night, even if I had to find out the date second-hand from someone who had been contracted to play.'

A groan escaped Rosalind's lips. She didn't want it to. She just wanted to lie very still with her eyes tight shut until the nightmare went away. A cool hand touched her forehead in a familiar gesture. 'She's very pale. Have you called a doctor?'

'Of course I've called the doctor.

He'll be here any moment.'

The door opened and Rose finally opened her eyes as her wrist was grasped by a professional and the doctor smiled down at her. 'This is no way to look after yourself, young lady. You should be at home with your feet up. I told you to take it easy for the first few months.'

'I'm sorry.'

'Well, I don't suppose there's much harm done.' He shone a light in her eyes. 'Did anyone see her fall? Did she knock her head?'

'She just sort of slithered to the floor. She'd had a bit of a shock,' Sarah said, tightly, and scowled at the perpetrator.

'I'm all right,' Rose protested. 'I'm fine. I just want to go home.' She tried to sit up, but the doctor stopped her.

'Best place for you, but just lie still for a moment while I take a look at you.'

He ushered everyone from the room, checked her over. When he was satisfied he opened the door. 'Mr Drayton? Will you come in?'

'No!' But Sarah and her parents melted away. Only Jack stood leaning against the door, white-faced, silent. She lay back and closed her eyes again, unable to bear it.

'Take her home, young man, and tuck her up in bed. You know where to call me if you have any worries. I know she'll be in capable hands.' He patted Rose's shoulder. 'I'll see you at the clinic next week. In the meantime, Rosalind, take it easy. No more gallivanting until we've delivered this little package safe and sound.'

'I wasn't gallivanting . . .'

'Goodnight to you both.' The door shut behind him and for a long while there was silence.

When she found the strength to open her eyes, Jack was still staring at her. 'Where's Harlowe,' he asked, quietly. 'He never seems to be around when he's needed.'

A tiny frown of concentration wrinkled her forehead. 'Why would Anthony be here? He doesn't like jazz.'

299

'So you came without him? Is it that bad already? Well, I did warn you.' The words were bitter.

Her head was throbbing and the light was still too bright. He wasn't making any sense, but it was too much effort to sort it out.

'Why are you here?' she demanded.

'I imagine the doctor assumed I'm the father of the child you're carrying. Hardly surprising, since he saw me with you day and night while you had the flu. He presumably thought we were living together. It doesn't matter. You can disabuse him when you attend his ante-natal clinic. It should give you both a good laugh.'

'Laugh?' She sat up. Too quickly. Swearing at her stupidity, he caught her and laid her back down. 'I don't know why you think it's funny, Jack,' she said, crossly, but her voice was too weak to have any impact. 'There is nothing funny about pregnancy. It's really very serious.'

'Reserve your complaints for your

husband.' He stood back, his eyes blanked of expression. 'I think I'd better go before he comes to collect you. I'm not in the mood to run into him right now.'

She pulled herself back up, fighting the dizziness. 'Jack!'

He turned, his fingers around the door handle, his voice cold as a glacier. 'I really don't think there's anything else left to say, do you?'

Temper flared dangerously. 'There's plenty left to say, Jack Drayton.' She had made it to her feet and stood clutching the end of the sofa, but the room was swaying about her.

'I'd like to help you, Rosie. But you left my bed to keep your promise to your precious Anthony. I should have remembered that you always keep your promises and you never made any to me. Not in words.' His face was livid against the black open-necked shirt, the dark hair. 'But I still don't understand how you could have done that. After the night we had spent together.' He took a step towards her. 'You still went to him. I tried to stop you. When I woke up, realised you'd gone, I came after you. But I was too late. You were already married.'

'So you left?' She said it almost to herself. It was true. She hadn't imagined it. He thought she had married Anthony. 'You went back to the Lodge and packed and left.' With understanding came hope, just a little of it, but enough to send her heart into an agitated clamour.

'Of course I left. What did you want me to do, stand around and cheer? Wish you luck? Throw a little confetti?'

'You should have. Oh, Jack, you should have.' She took a step towards him, held out her hands. 'Hold me.'

He seized her shoulders, kept her at arms length. 'What sort of game is this, Rosie? You made your decision. It's too late to change your mind. I have strict rules about messing with other men's wives.'

'Noble.' She smiled. 'I said so.'

His face creased with concern as her legs finally gave up the unequal task and began to buckle beneath her and he swung her into her arms and laid her once more on the sofa.

'Are you all right?' he asked anxiously. 'Shall I get the doctor back. He may not have left.'

'I don't need a doctor, Jack. I just need you.'

He looked haunted. For the first time she noticed how drawn he looked. Hollow-eyed. 'Rosie, please don't — '

She reached up and placed one finger across his lips. 'I didn't marry Anthony Harlowe. Do you hear me? When I met him in the Napier it was to explain that I couldn't marry him after all because I had fallen in love with someone else.' That sounded very bold. But this was no time for games. No time to take a chance that he might not understand. 'He, poor love, was thoroughly relieved. He had been thrown into Julie's company — '

'Julie?'

'My secretary. You've met her at the office. Thirtyish, fair hair, about my height?'

'What about her?'

'When I was sick Anthony saw rather a lot of her.' She giggled. 'In fact, I had the impression from Julie that he saw all of her. Not that it matters, because he married her instead of me.'

'You're not married . . . ' He looked as if he had been hit with a sandbag. 'But I saw you . . . '

'You saw Julie. I promised her I would go to the ceremony. She didn't want anyone to think I was resentful that Anthony had dumped me. She has a tidy mind.'

'It was her I saw him kissing? I only saw his face; she was hidden behind some vast headgear.' He took her hand in his, bare of any rings, still not quite able to believe what he was hearing. 'I don't understand. But why on earth did you keep up the pretence if it was all over?' He touched the small jagged scar on his cheek. 'Hadn't you hurt me enough?'

'I wasn't trying to hurt you, Jack. I was trying to save myself. But I don't believe I ever stood a chance. I was a novice playing the games master.'

He lifted her fingers to his lips and kissed them. 'You underrate yourself, my love. There's a great deal to be said for untutored enthusiasm.' He very gently, almost fearfully, laid his hand upon her abdomen. 'Then this is mine? Truly?'

She nodded and in the most tender, most heart-touching gesture, he bent and kissed her there.

'Will you marry me, Rosie?' he asked.

'Because of the baby?'

'No, because I love you. Because I fell in love with a photograph of a laughing red-headed girl very early one morning in a bar in New Orleans. We had played, we had talked and we had got drunk. Rich started to tell me about his family. How he missed them, how he could never go back. How you could never go back. I didn't understand that. Not until I woke up and found myself alone and the girl I loved apparently married to someone else.'

'You saw my picture and came to look for me?' she asked, stunned.

'Oh, yes, my love, I came to look for you and Rich made it easy. It was your birthday soon, he said. Could I call and say hello from your Dada?'

'He told me that.'

'And there you were. Not a girl any more. More lovely, more desirable. A woman. A woman about to marry someone else.'

'For a life of comfort and ease?' she felt sure enough now, to tease him a little.

'It seemed likely. You can hardly blame me for thinking it.'

'You were wrong, Jack. I was going to marry Anthony because he offered emotional security. He would never walk away . . .'

'No?' he asked. 'Then what's he doing married to someone else?'

'I was the one who walked away, Jack.'

'Why?' There was an urgency about the question.

'Because ... because I heard a 'different drummer' ... '

'Can't you say it?' he demanded, then sighed and scooped her up and sat with her in his arms, holding her close. 'Will you marry me, Rosie?' She would have spoken but he stopped her. 'Not because of the baby. Simply because you want to. I've thought of nothing else, day or night, for weeks, but holding you in my arms like this and hoping that you would love me in return. I love you. I want you to be my wife.' He stroked the rich chestnut curls back from her forehead. 'I know I behaved like an idiot, my darling. But you insisted you were going to marry Harlowe and that seemed to take a certain cold-bloodedness when I could see with one eye closed that you weren't in love with him.'

'I thought I was until I met you, wretch.'

He laughed. 'Do you know, I actually believe you. But at the time I didn't much relish the thought of being snapped up by a fortune-hunter as a better prospect. Not even one I was in love with. Can you understand that? Was I mad to expect you to throw him up for a penniless nobody? Just for love?'

'Crazy. But I did. And within five minutes of doing it, I discovered you had been playing me for a fool.'

'No, love, I was the fool.'

'Then, fool, I love you.'

'Truly?'

'I tried to stop, when you went away. I thought it would help with the pain. But it made no difference.'

'And you would have had my baby, on your own? Why on earth didn't Rich tell me? He must have been ready to do murder.'

'For about five minutes. But he didn't know where you were.'

He laughed. 'I think he must have had a good idea. Or why would he have booked a musician we both loathe? Someone who would have broken his neck to tell me he was going to play in my club?'

'He promised!'

'And a Parry promise is made to keep, I know. But he is your father.' He was suddenly serious. 'Will you have me, Rosie?' A tap at the door interrupted her answer. 'Wait!' he commanded.

'That might be my father now,' she warned, with a teasing smile.

'Then you'd better say yes quickly, in case he decides to become thoroughly Victorian and break the door down.'

'Yes,' she said. 'Please.' And she put her arms around his neck and kissed him and when Rich Parry finally opened the door neither of them heard him and he closed it again and went away.

We do hope that you have enjoyed reading this large print book.

Did you know that all of our titles are available for purchase?

We publish a wide range of high quality large print books including:
Romances, Mysteries, Classics
General Fiction
Non Fiction and Westerns

Special interest titles available in large print are:
The Little Oxford Dictionary
Music Book, Song Book
Hymn Book, Service Book

Also available from us courtesy of Oxford University Press:
Young Readers' Dictionary
(large print edition)
Young Readers' Thesaurus
(large print edition)

For further information or a free brochure, please contact us at:
Ulverscroft Large Print Books Ltd.,
The Green, Bradgate Road, Anstey,
Leicester, LE7 7FU, England.
Tel: (00 44) **0116 236 4325**
Fax: (00 44) **0116 234 0205**

FALSE PRETENCES

Phyllis Humphrey

When Ginger Maddox, a San Francisco stock-broker, meets handsome Neil Cameron, she becomes attracted to him. But then mysterious things begin to happen, involving Neil's aunts. After a romantic weekend with Neil, Ginger overhears a telephone conversation confirming her growing suspicions that he's involved in illegal trading. She's devastated, fearing that this could end their relationship. But it's the elderly aunts who help show the young people that love will find a way.

CUCKOO IN THE NEST

Joyce Johnson

On his deathbed, reclusive million-aire Sir Harry Trevain asks his beloved granddaughter, Daisy, to restore harmony to their fractured family. But as the Trevain family gathers for Sir Harry's funeral, tensions are already surfacing. Then, at the funeral, a handsome stranger arrives from America claiming to be Sir Harry's grandson. The family is outraged, but Daisy, true to her promise to her grandfather, wel-comes the stranger to Pencreek and finds herself irresistibly drawn to Ben Trevain . . .

'I'LL BE THERE FOR YOU'

Chrissie Loveday

Amy returns home to find the house deserted and her father mysteriously absent. Her oldest friend Greg rallies round and they begin their mission to find her father. Had her father planned some sort of surprise holiday for her? Or was there a sinister purpose behind the mysterious phone calls? Mystery, adventure, possible danger and a trip to Southern Spain follow. But how could they enjoy the beautiful settings with such threats hanging over them?

JANE I'M-STILL-SINGLE JONES

Joan Reeves

Despite her ownership of a successful business in New York, Jane Louise Jones is nervous about her impending high school reunion in Vernon, Louisiana. There she must wear a badge emblazoned with her unmarried status, which Morgan Sherwood might see. Unbelievably handsome and now rich, Morgan had broken her heart in the senior year. Meanwhile, Morgan plans to make her fall in love with him all over again, he's never forgotten their passionate kisses — and now he wants more . . .